# TUESDAY NIGHT FOOTBALL

# TUESDAY NIGHT FOOTBALL

### A NOVEL

by Alex Karras
and Douglas Graham

A BIRCH LANE PRESS BOOK
*Published by Carol Publishing Group*

A Birch Lane Press Book
Published by Carol Publishing Group
Birch Lane Press is registered trademark of
Carol Communications, Inc.

Editorial Offices          Sales & Distribution Offices
600 Madison Avenue         120 Enterprise Avenue
New York, NY 10022         Secaucus, NJ 07094

In Canada: Musson Book Company
A division of General Publishing Co. Limited
Don Mills, Ontario

Queries regarding rights and permissions
should be addressed to: Carol Publishing Group,
600 Madison Avenue, New York, NY 10022

"The Everything Corporation Jingle," words and music by
J. Bruce Langhorne. Copyright © 1991 by J. Bruce Langhorne.
Used by permission.

Manufactured in the United States of America
10 9 8 7 6 5 4 3 2 1

Carol Publishing Group books are available at special discounts
for bulk purchases, for sales promotions, fund raising, or
educational purposes. Special editions can also be created to
specifications. For details contact: Special Sales Department,
Carol Publishing Group, 120 Enterprise Ave., Secaucus, NJ 07094

**Library of Congress Cataloging-in-Publication Data**

Karras, Alex.
    Tuesday night football : a novel / by Alex Karras and Douglas
Graham.
       p.   cm.
    "A Birch Lane Press book."
    ISBN 1–55972–081–6
    I. Graham, Douglas.  II. Title.
PS3561.A6935T8   1991
813'.54—dc20                                        94–4260
                                                    CIP

# CONTENTS

# TUESDAY
# NIGHT
# FOOTBALL

**PART ONE**

# The World Through the Eyes of Lazlo

# ONE

Lately I've been thinking a lot about my old friend Lazlo Horvath. For some reason, every time I turn on the television set, Lazlo pops into my mind. I find myself wondering where he is and what he's doing now. With Lazlo anything's possible.

I've met a lot of strange people in my life, but I've never known anybody quite like Lazlo. The first thing I noticed was that everything about him was wrong. He was a giant who never quite grew into his body, so there was an awkwardness about him, like a kid who grows eight inches in one summer and is always tripping over his own feet. And he was a *terrible* dresser, with absolutely no sense of taste, style or color. And, because he was so big, none of his clothes ever fit him properly, which made him look even more ridiculous. He could give Brooks Brothers a bad name. Clothing manufacturers should have paid him not to wear their fashions.

3

But none of that mattered to Lazlo. He had more important things on his mind, like being happy.

And Lazlo Horvath was the happiest man in the world.

I think I know what you're thinking. You're thinking that only an idiot is happy all the time. Some people have even mistaken Lazlo for an idiot, but that's only because they were so tied up in knots by their own unhappiness that they couldn't believe it was possible for anybody to be anything else. They were so caught up in money and power and deals and ego and image that they could never grasp what Lazlo knew in his heart: that being happy is better than being miserable. You don't have to be an idiot to be happy; in fact, it might even be the other way around.

Naturally some people were threatened by Lazlo. Someone else's happiness can be a very threatening thing to one who's not prepared for it. In fact, if everyone in the world were genuinely happy, most of our biggest industries would be out of business, which would make a lot of people unhappy.

Lazlo knew that not everyone liked him, but that didn't make him unhappy either. Everyone who really knew him liked him, and for those who didn't, well, he just assumed that their problem wasn't with *him*, really, but with themselves, and of course he was right. He had no desire to change them, or anything in the world, for that matter. Not that the world was perfect. On the contrary. Lazlo read the papers and watched the news, so he knew as well as the next person how screwed up everything was. And if he thought about it for a long time it would start to make him unhappy (for Lazlo truly loved people, and wanted everyone to be as happy as he was). But then he would realize that there wasn't a single thing he could do about it. The problems of the world were totally out of his control, best left to a higher authority. Let God take care of the world, he'd say, because that's God's job. He's equipped for it. He knows how to do it. Lazlo's job is to be happy. And, reminding himself of how lucky he was just to be alive and to be Lazlo, he would soon be happy again.

He preferred to experience the world as a magical place, full of wonder and endless possibilities, and who could blame him? Is it so wrong to look for the good in everything, to live out your dreams, to leave the judging to God? In this respect Lazlo was a huge, overgrown child who lived in a fantasy world that never disappointed him. Whether it was a blessing or a curse I don't know, but to Lazlo it made no difference. It just *was,* and it was all right with him.

# TWO

Lazlo learned at the age of eleven that he wasn't cool. His friend Wojciech told him. They were walking through a salvage yard in Hamtramk, watching them crush old cars into steel cubes. Wojciech, who was fifteen, reached in his pocket for a pack of Lucky Strikes, took one out and lit it, cupping his hand expertly so the wind wouldn't blow out the match. Lazlo watched this ritual with a kind of awe. Wojciech inhaled deeply, then exhaled, sending a billow of blue smoke skyward. Two ribbons of smoke even came through Wojciech's nose. Lazlo was truly impressed. When it came to smoking, Wojciech was an old pro.

"How come you smoke? asked Lazlo. He wasn't being judgmental; he just wanted information.

"'Cause *every*body smokes," shrugged Wojciech. "'Cause it's *cool*, that's why. I dunno."

Lazlo had to admit that his friend Wojciech was cool. Standing there in his varsity jacket with the black leather sleeves, his slicked-back "duck's ass" Elvis Presley-style hair-cut and real Italian shoes with pointed toes and stiletto heels, Wojciech was probably the coolest guy in the neighborhood. Maybe in all of Hamtramk. The only reason he let Lazlo hang out with him was because Lazlo was so big, even at eleven, that the other kids wouldn't mess with him when Lazlo was along. Besides, it gave Wojciech somebody to instruct in the ways of the world. Doctor Cool.

"I never smoked in my life," said Lazlo, just as Wojciech blew a chain of perfect smoke rings.

"That's 'cause you're not cool," said Wojciech matter-of-factly. "It's not *my* fault you're a dipshit."

"So, do you think you could teach me?" asked Lazlo.

"Teach you what? To be cool? Jesus, Lazlo, that would take a million years."

"No," said Lazlo. "Just teach me how to smoke. You know. The right way. So I can get it to come out through my nose, like you do."

Wojciech thought about this for a minute, then agreed. "Okay, why not. Here," he said, taking out another cigarette and handing it to Lazlo, "the first thing you gotta do is learn how to hold it so you don't look like a weenie."

Lazlo studied the little cigarette he clutched in his huge, meaty hand.

"LSMFT," he said. "Lucky Strike means fine tobacco. So round, so firm, so fully packed..."

"Cut the commercial, Lazlo," said Wojciech, who was growing impatient. "You wanna smoke or dontcha?"

"Yeah, I wanna smoke!" said Lazlo. He really didn't want to any more, but it was too late for him to back out now.

Wojciech showed him how to hold the cigarette to get the maximum cool effect. He showed him how to light it and look cool doing it. He showed him how to inhale, slowly and deeply, being careful not to swallow the smoke. Swallowing the smoke was definitely not cool. Then it was Lazlo's turn.

Lazlo held the cigarette in his mouth while Wojciech, cupping his hands, very coolly lit it for him. Lazlo took a drag—long and slow, just as he'd been instructed—and inhaled deeply. So far, so good. Wojciech watched approvingly, with just the slightest trace of a smile on his lips, like maybe he knew something Lazlo didn't.

When the blast came, two or three seconds later, it came with the fury of a runaway freight train. As the smoke reached poor Lazlo's lungs, he felt like he'd been hit by a cannonball at close range. His eyes bugged out like a bullfrog's, his cheeks puffed, his knees buckled, hot flashes sent his head spinning and his skin turned the most disgusting shade of yellow ever seen in Hamtramk. Wojciech started laughing uncontrollably, which made Lazlo feel even worse. He swallowed some of the smoke and began to gag. His head reeled. He knew he was going to die as punishment for smoking that cigarette; he just hoped it would happen soon.

With every one of Lazlo's contortions Wojciech became more hysterical. He laughed so hard he fell to his knees, pointing the finger of humiliation at the victim of his instruction. Doctor Cool's face was streaked with tears as he guffawed.

By now Lazlo was also on his knees, but he wasn't laughing. His coughing became the sound of geese honking, which was the funniest thing Wojciech had ever heard. Lazlo choked, farted, honked and puked until every trace of cigarette smoke was finally expelled from every orifice of his oversized eleven-year-old body.

Far from killing Lazlo, it was the greatest thing that ever happened to him. It changed his life forever. Because at that moment, heaving up his guts in a godforsaken Hamtramk junkyard, he realized something that most of us never learn even if we live to be a hundred:

It is not necessary to be cool to be happy.

And with that simple understanding, a tremendous burden was suddenly lifted from him, and he never needed to be cool after that.

# THREE

**L**azlo wasn't a great student. Naturally his teachers decided that there must be something wrong with him—there had to be, because if there wasn't something wrong with *him,* then there had to be something wrong with *them.* And teachers, as we all know, are never wrong. So they tested him to see what it was that was wrong.

They could have saved themselves (and Lazlo, too) a lot of trouble just by talking to him. Because what was "wrong" with Lazlo doesn't show up on tests. It was exactly the same thing that's wrong with a lot of kids: School was a drag. It was incredibly boring. There was nothing in any textbook that could begin to compare with the fantastic Technicolor adventures that went on in his head, every day, morning 'til night. The academic world of math and science and "see Spot run" had no place in Lazlo's daydreams. School was a prison sentence for him.

But there was a wonderful new invention in those days,

and it was called television. To Lazlo it was nothing less than an Aladdin's lamp—a magic box that, just by his turning a knob, connected him with all the wonders of the outside world, excited his imagination and, most of all, promised him that he would never have to be lonely again. Television became his best and most loyal friend, and from the beginning he believed everything it told him.

And why not? After all, television was his real teacher. The very first time he ever laid eyes on a television set he didn't speak a word of English. In fact, for the first three years of his life he didn't speak at all, because he was very confused.

To understand Lazlo's problem we have to go back a little bit.

His father, Janos, was a proud, stubborn little man who had been a fire-eater in the Hungarian circus. It was there that he met Dagmar, who would later become his wife and, eventually, Lazlo's mother. Dagmar was a brainless beauty who stood a full foot taller than Janos. Her job was to ride around the ring on an elephant, dressed only in a bathing suit. (Dagmar was dressed in the bathing suit; not the elephant.) She was sought after and pursued by every man in the circus troupe except Janos, who was too busy scorching his tonsils to notice her. Besides, being a modest man, Janos was sure that he didn't stand a chance with such a legendary beauty as Dagmar, so he didn't even try. But Dagmar wasn't interested in any of the others, not even the Croatian aerialist who plunged ninety feet to his death in a vain and stupid attempt to impress her by performing without a safety net. No, it was Janos she wanted, and it was Janos she got. (It shouldn't surprise you that beautiful women almost always get what they think they want.)

They were married by the mayor of Budapest in the center ring of the circus in front of six hundred witnesses. That night Janos ate fire like he had never eaten fire before, and Dagmar, always playing to the crowd, was a sight to behold as she went through her whole elephant routine still wearing her white lace wedding dress. Janos loved her. The audience loved her. All of Hungary loved her! It was the happiest night of he life, and her greatest performance ever. Lazlo still has the pictures.

Not long after that the war broke out, and nothing was quite the same. There was very little joy in Hungary, or anywhere else in Europe, for that matter. Dagmar and Janos felt robbed of something they didn't even know could be lost, something they couldn't explain. Oh, they still had each other, and were still very much in love. And they still had their work with the circus. On the surface not that much had changed. But the Hungarian spirit goes far deeper than the surface. It was as though all the birds in Budapest had suddenly stopped singing. Now whenever they performed, they performed, not for rowdy friends, but for humorless German officers in gray uniforms who applauded politely and gave nothing else back. With each performance they would go through the motions with fake smiles and forced enthusiasm, because the consequences of failure were too horrible to imagine. The circus they loved became a job they began to dread.

"Those fucking Nazis," Janos would say, but very quietly, and only to Dagmar.

Then Lazlo came along. The minute Dagmar found out she was pregnant, she quit riding elephants and started setting up a nursery. Janos couldn't have been happier, and for a while even forgot how much he hated those "fucking Nazis"; he was going to be a papa. Somehow life goes on after all.

War or no war, Janos was determined to provide the best for his son. And when the Nazis finally surrendered, the world looked a whole lot brighter. Janos and Dagmar, with baby Lazlo in tow, were out in the streets with everyone else to welcome their Russian liberators. But the celebration didn't last long. Tanks are tanks. Sometimes only the colors of the uniforms change.

Janos wasn't a political person, but it didn't take him long to read the writing on the wall. "Those fucking Russians," he would say, but very quietly, and only to Dagmar. He knew they had to get out of Hungary if his son Lazlo was to have any chance at all. So in the middle of then night they crossed the border into occupied Austria and began the long journey to America, leaving the Old World and all of its problems behind forever.

# FOUR

**A**t the first sight of the Statue of Liberty, Dagmar burst out crying, as much for the uncertainty of what lay ahead as for the life she could never go back to. Janos, who (as we know) was a proud man, didn't believe in public displays of emotion. He quietly swallowed the lump in his throat as he squeezed Dagmar's hand there on the deck of the ship. Lazlo gurgled and smiled serenely, completely unaware of the profound significance of this entire adventure. He didn't know where he was or where he'd been. He didn't know anything about the Nazis or the Russians or the war that had just ended. He didn't know about America or the Statue of Liberty, or even Tuesday Night Football. He only knew that he was Lazlo and that he was happy at that precise moment; he didn't know why and he certainly didn't care. He was so happy that he peed in his pants, which of course made him even happier.

Suddenly, Janos became very solemn, which he often did on important occasions. Dagmar was used to it by now.

"Dagmar," he said solemnly, "now that we are in America we must do as the Americans. In fact, we must *become* Americans. I have therefore decided that from this day on we will speak only English, even when we are alone."

Dagmar looked at him like he was crazy. "But Janos, we don't *know* any English," she said. (She was right; they didn't.)

"My point exactly," said Janos with cryptic finality.

"What about Lazlo?" Dagmar wanted to know.

"*Especially* Lazlo. He must learn to be an American, too. We will speak to him in English or not at all."

Dagmar didn't appreciate being bossed around by Janos. (If she really *had* been an American woman, she probably would have told him to go fuck himself in the language of her choice.) But she was just a Magyar peasant girl from northern Hungary who rode elephants and had been brought up to obey her husband, no matter how pigheaded he might be. So she reluctantly agreed to speak only English, even when they were alone.

As for Lazlo, giving up Hungarian for English shouldn't have been a big deal. He was barely a year old and didn't even know what he *was,* let alone what language he was supposed to speak. But since his parents had agreed to speak English or nothing at all, most of the time they spoke nothing at all.

Until he was three years old Lazlo just assumed that they stopped talking to him because they didn't like him anymore. Still, he wasn't about to let that prevent him from being happy.

# FIVE

**J**anos and Dagmar couldn't wait to write to their friends back in Hungary and tell them what they had discovered. In America you could go where you wanted, you could live where you wanted, you could work where you wanted. You could even *say* what you wanted. America had hamburgers and Coca-Cola, Frank Sinatra records, and movies for a dime. America had grocery stores that actually had food on the shelves, and plenty of it; you didn't have to stand on line to buy bread or anything else. And there were huge department stores with everything anyone could ever want. Yes, America was at the top of the heap in those days—the richest, freest and most powerful nation on earth—production lines rolling, everybody working, everybody buying. The lowliest workers in America all seemed to have things that the richest person in Budapest could never even dream of: shiny new cars, electric stoves, refrigerators, phonographs, radios, telephones. America was Consumer Paradise.

Janos (who prided himself on his logical ability) decided that the first step to becoming an American was to become a consumer. The more things you buy, the better American you are. And, like any child in a toy store, he wanted just about everything he saw.

But having all those things takes money, even in America, and there weren't a lot of jobs in those days for Hungarian fire-eaters (or beautiful elephant girls). So Janos and Dagmar bundled up baby Lazlo and set out to find work in Detroit, the teeming center of the industrial universe, the very symbol of America's boundless prosperity.

They wound up in Hamtramk instead.

Try to imagine Lazlo's confusion: First his very own mother and father decide not to talk to him at all except in English, a language they don't know the first thing about; then they end up in the one place in the United States where virtually everybody speaks Polish and English is *still* a foreign language. If a neighbor lady happened to stop Dagmar on the street while she was out with Lazlo and said, "My, what a sweet little boy!" Dagmar would just nod and smile and move on; she wouldn't know what the woman had said, but she would assume it was some kind of compliment. But to Lazlo, looking up from his stroller, "My, what a sweet little boy" sounded like "OJEJKU, JAKI SŁODKI MALUTKI CHŁOP-CZK," which of course meant absolutely nothing to him and might just as well have been Martian.

Not that Hamtramk was Mars; actually it was almost pleasant in a weird sort of way—tree-shaded streets lined with wood-frame tract houses, manicured lawns (many with ceramic pink flamingos, birdbaths and year-round nativity scenes), mom-and-pop groceries, and St. Ladislaus Catholic church where the Sunday sermons were still delivered in Polish. Plump little women wearing babushkas could be seen padding to market every day, old-country relics caught in a New World time warp. There was Jerzy's barber shop and the

Krakow Bar on Joseph Campau Avenue where two and three generations of Polish men would go on Saturdays to get away from their wives, mothers and daughters for a while, to trade war stories, to bitch about their jobs, to brag about their children, to reminisce about better days gone by, and to solve the problems of the world over a haircut or a pitcher of beer. There was the Polish-American Hall on Caniff Road where every Friday night you could polka 'til you puked to the piston beat of Mirek Celinski and his Fabulous Polecats. (At that time Mirek was the undisputed accordion champion of Hamtramk, constantly surrounded by polka groupies. He was a legend in the community, revered as much for his prowess with the women as for his amazing dexterity on the Hohner. If it weren't for Mirek, Lazlo certainly wouldn't be where he is today, but I'll get to that later.)

To the Poles who lived there, Hamtramk was a state of mind—a tiny slice of the homeland they loved—a sanctuary where they could preserve something of their culture before it disappeared altogether within the Great American Melting Pot. It was a link to their past and an investment in their future. It was an extended family that made its own rules and settled its own scores. It was Warsaw in exile.

To Detroiters, whose city surrounded Hamtramk, it was total chaos, a blue-collar snake pit where people got into fistfights over parking spaces (and the men were even tougher), a place where all the street signs were incomprehensible, where you didn't go unless you wanted to become hopelessly lost behind enemy lines.

To Lazlo, the only Hungarian kid in Hamtramk, it was simply wonderful—a banquet of brand new sights and sounds and smells in a land of excitable giants. It was a non-stop movie; he didn't quite understand it, but he knew that he never wanted it to end.

# SIX

One day, when Lazlo was about two, his father came home behind the wheel of a gleaming new car. (Actually it was a nine-year-old Studebaker coupe with a lot of rust on the rocker panels, but to Lazlo it was the biggest, shiniest, fastest, most beautiful car in the whole world.) Janos pulled the car right up into the driveway and began honking the horn until Dagmar and Lazlo came out of the house to see what the commotion was, as did several neighbors. The sight of the Studebaker with Janos in it took Dagmar's breath away; she started to cry, just as she had done when she first saw the Statue of Liberty. Lazlo clutched his mother's leg and looked up at her plaintively, wondering what was wrong. Then he saw his father jump out of the car and rush toward them, smiling and laughing and waving a piece of paper in his hand. Lazlo was perplexed; it didn't make any sense for one to be so happy and the other to be so sad over a dumb Studebaker.

19

"Dagmar, he's beauteous, no?!" shouted Janos in his best pidgin English, gesturing toward the car. "What you *tink*, Dagmar? You like him?"

"Yes, he's very nice," Dagmar agreed. There was hesitation in her voice.

"And he is belonging to *us* now!" said Janos, showing her the paper.

"But Janos, how we *pay* for such a ting?"

"The *bank* pay already," explained Janos. "Then each month we give bank a little bit of monies."

"You must return the car, Janos, before they find out you took it."

"I *can't* return him, Dagmar. I already told you, he is belonging to *us* now!" He showed her the paper again. "This is how they do it in America."

Lazlo watched as she took the official-looking paper from him and read it aloud, trying to understand all the unfamiliar words. Finally she came to the part where it said "Janos Horvath" and let out a drum-splitting shriek. She grabbed Janos, pulling him into a bear hug, then began to jump up and down like on a pogo stick, the two of them bouncing and turning round and round with Lazlo in the center like a miniature maypole. Dagmar and Janos were both laughing now, and Lazlo, satisfied that everything was all right again, laughed along with them. Never had he seen them so happy, which made him even happier than he usually was.

"You know what this means, Dagmar?" effused Janos. "This means that we are real Americans now, just like everybody else!"

It was Lazlo's first lesson in commerce, and what an impression it made! He had seen his grumpy, humorless, hard-working father suddenly transformed into a loving, joyous, completely fulfilled human being, dancing and laughing with his mother out there on the sidewalk in front of

God and everybody, and all because the Detroit Bank & Trust had agreed to float a $400 loan for a 1938 Studebaker coupe.

He wished that everybody could have a Studebaker; then everybody would be happy like his father.

That night they all went for a ride in the new (used) car. It was the first time Lazlo had ever been in an automobile and only the second time he could remember being out after dark. Lazlo sat on his mother's lap as they drove along Conant Avenue toward downtown Detroit and the river, jerking and stalling at every traffic signal. (Janos was a terrible driver; he never bothered with the American formality of acquiring a driver's license.) Lazlo paid no attention to his father's driving. His eyes were riveted on the electric signs and billboards that lit up the night, pitching every product imaginable, commanding his attention. There was Elsie the Borden Cow with a fifteen-foot mechanical head that moved slowly back and forth while her mouth chewed in perfect rhythm; there was a gigantic picture of a pudgy-faced little girl eating a Hostess cupcake, which was one of Lazlo's favorite things to begin with; there was a Goodyear tire that had to be fifty feet tall and was actually spinning, though it wasn't going anywhere; there were billboards for Wonder Bread, Stroh's Beer, Vernor's Ginger Ale, and Coca-Cola, where the lights made the bottle appear to fiz; there was a woman who looked like a movie star, blowing smoke rings from her Camel cigarette (which may be where Wojciech later got the idea); there were smiling young couples with their new Hudsons, DeSotos, Fords and Chevies, all of them just as happy as he'd just seen his parents that very afternoon; there was the Kowalski Quality Sausage factory (where his mother worked as a sausage stuffer) and, a block down the street, an enormous neon flying red horse whose wings really seemed to flap. The Mobiloil steed soared into the blackness of the Detroit sky, and Lazlo's spirit soared right along with it.

# SEVEN

The boy don't talk. He's almost three years old and still he don't talk. What is wrong with him, anyhow?" Janos was carrying on like a man who had just discovered that his son hadn't said a word in his whole life. Dagmar tried to calm him.

"Maybe he don't have nuttink to say."

"Or maybe he's a little dumb in the head," said Janos, who always had to have the last word on everything.

But they were both wrong. Lazlo wasn't dumb in the head, and he had plenty to say. He just hadn't figured out how to say it yet. So far he'd spent all of his time watching and listening—and waiting. Eventually he *would* speak, but not until he was totally clear on the concept. There would be time to say everything that had to be said. What he needed now were just the *right* words that would make everybody happy.

They took him to a doctor, who pronounced him perfectly healthy.

"Seems fine to me," said the doctor.

"Then why he don't talk to us?" asked Janos.

"Do you ever talk to *him?*"

Janos and Dagmar looked at each other. Lazlo looked at both of them, waiting for their answer. He wanted to see how truthful they would be.

"Not so much, I guess," Dagmar admitted finally. "We are boat working all the time." Janos nodded his head in reluctant agreement. Lazlo laughed his bubbly laugh and clapped his little hands together; they had passed the test and he was happy that these two honest people were his parents, even if they didn't talk to him.

"Well, you ought to try talking to him once in a while," said the doctor. "Children aren't pets, you know. They need attention."

*You tell 'em, Doc!* Lazlo would have said if he could talk. *Good for you! I'm not a pet, I'm Lazlo! And I sure could use some attention.* But since he couldn't talk, all he could do was *think* those things and smile his biggest smile to let everybody know that he knew exactly what was going on. Lazlo liked this doctor because he remembered what it was like to be three. (Anybody who thinks it's easy being three is either crazy or has never been three.)

"Don't worry. He'll talk when he gets around to it," said the doctor, "and then you'll probably wish he didn't." (This doctor prided himself on a wry sense of humor.) He charged them ten dollars for the visit, and Janos complained about it all the way home while Lazlo stared out the window, studying all the billboards on Woodward Avenue.

"That fucking doctor, who he tink he is anyhow?" said Janos as he weaved in and out of traffic. "He wants we should quit our jobs and talk to *Lazlo?* How is he expecting us to keep it up with the Jones family? Is he fucking nuts or what?"

But the doctor wasn't the real problem. The real problem was that Janos was beginning to feel like a failure as a father because his son wouldn't talk to him. He shouldn't have taken it personally; Lazlo didn't talk to anybody.

And Janos had a point: It wasn't easy "keeping it up with the Jones family," which (in his mind) was absolutely necessary if you wanted to live in America. That's why he worked night and day, often putting in double shifts at the Dodge main assembly plant. (Because of his vast experience with fire they made him a welder, and he quickly advanced from apprentice to journeyman. He also improved his English; in no time at all he was able to master such useful expressions as, "This goddam U-joint is no fucking good," and everyone would know exactly what he was talking about and fix the "goddamn U-joint."

As hard as he worked, though, it still wasn't enough. So Dagmar had to work too, stuffing kielbasa skins with God-knows-what for $1.05 an hour at the Kowalski Quality Sausage factory. It was the kind of mindless job she could handle (even less challenging than riding around a circus ring on a drugged-up old elephant), and besides, they needed the money if they were going to be real Americans.

So Lazlo hardly ever saw them. What he saw instead was Mrs. Kluzewski, an enormous woman with huge, pendulous breasts (like underinflated footballs) who always smelled of cooked cabbage and beets. In Lazlo's land of the giants, Mrs. Kluzewski was the undisputed empress—the most feared and dreaded of all grownups: The babysitter.

# EIGHT

**E**very day was the same. Mrs. Kluzewski would arrive and Lazlo's parents would kiss him on his forehead and leave for work. (He would stare up mournfully at them as they were going out the door, hoping that just once they would stay home and play with him, or at least talk to him; they never did.) Then, once they were gone, Mrs. Kluzewski would take over his life with all the authority and warmth of a Russian commissar.

"Have you been good boy, Lazlo?" she would always ask as soon as his parents had left. (Of *course* he'd been a good boy. How could a three-year-old with absolutely nothing to do and no one to talk to be anything *but* a good boy? He never even *complained*, for chrissake!) But he wouldn't answer, and Mrs. Kluzewski would go about her daily routine, completely ignoring him until it was time to go to the park, where she would meet her friends and exchange gossip in that strange Martian language that Lazlo didn't understand. (He was convinced that she didn't want him to know what they were talking about, in case he ever decided to speak and would spill the beans. What kinds of secrets were these giant women keeping from him?)

Lazlo didn't like the park. It occurred to him that the whole idea of going to the park was so that he could play with other kids and get a little exercise, but that's not what Mrs. Kluzewski had in mind. In the first place, she always rolled him there in a stroller, which was humiliating for a boy his size who was perfectly capable of walking. No exercise there. Then, once they arrived, he was never allowed to wander more than five feet away, let alone play with the other kids on the slides or the monkey bars. (This wasn't a conscious act of meanness on Mrs. K's part; she, like most people, just *assumed* that Lazlo was a little goofy, and she didn't want to be responsible if he fell off the monkey bars and broke his neck.)

Lazlo didn't know any of this. All he knew was that he felt like a dog on an invisible leash, and he remembered what the doctor had said about children not being pets. But if he tried to go where the action was, he was soon apprehended by the iron hand of Mrs. Kluzewski and returned to his place of confinement under the elm tree near the bench where Mrs. K and her giant matronly cronies yacked on and on until lunchtime. He would sit and stare at the sky, wondering what kind of world lay beyond the grassy expanse of the park and those belching black smokestacks in the distance. Was it the world of happy people that he saw that night on all the billboards? Why were they so happy? What were they trying to tell him? What did it all mean? These were difficult questions for a three-year-old, but Lazlo decided that he would find out what their secret was and embrace it as his own. One day *he* would be one of those happy people on a neon billboard, and wouldn't Mrs. Kluzewski be surprised! And he would think about this day after day, for hours on

end, every time he went to the park, because there was
nothing else for him to do there.

Then suddenly, as if on cue, everyone would disperse.
The formless female giants would all stand up and leave,
going in separate directions, their business of the day concluded. And, without a word, Mrs. K would pack Lazlo
snugly into his stroller and wheel him home again like a little
invalid for all the world to laugh at or to pity—he didn't know
which was worse.

After lunch Mrs. Kluzewski would send Lazlo to his
room for his afternoon nap, then she would turn on the radio
to listen to her "stories"—"Ma Perkins," "Pepper Young's
Family" and "Helen Trent." Instead of sleeping, Lazlo would
open the bedroom door and listen along with her. At first he
couldn't figure out how all those people got inside that little
box, but he knew they were in there because he could hear
their voices. And he didn't know what they were saying,
exactly, because the stories were *very* complicated and went
on forever. But he did know that the people inside the radio
didn't seem to be very happy (maybe it was because they were
struck inside that box, like Lazlo was stuck in his room; at
least they could talk to each other, he thought). But sometimes those voices would stop, and they would be replaced by
happy voices (and happy music) talking and singing about, of
all things, soap: *Ivory Snow* ("Ninety-nine and forty-four one-
hundredths percent pure") or *Ajax* ("Use Ajax, the foaming
cleanser—bah-bah-boom-boom-boom-boom-boom—floats
the dirt right down the drain—bah-bah-boom-boom-boom-
boom-boom!"). Every kind of soap. And sometimes they sang
about soup ("Mm-mm good, mm-mm good, that's what
Campbell's soups are, mm-mm good!").

It wasn't always easy for Lazlo to distinguish between
*soap* and *soup,* but he definitely liked all those voices; they
were the friendliest voices he'd ever heard, and they never

failed to make him happy. He wondered if they were the same people he saw on the billboards. If so, he wanted to be just like them some day.

# NINE

Long before there was Tuesday Night Football, there were the Friday Night Fights, televised live from Madison Square Garden in New York. Janos (who was basically a coward and had never been in a fight in his life) was a rabid boxing fan who liked to consider himself somewhat of an authority on prizefighting. So every Friday night he and some of his buddies from the plant would go down to Casimir's Bar on Wyandotte Avenue where they would drink pitchers of Miller High Life with shots of Jack Daniels and watch the bouts on Casimir's television set, a twelve-inch Motorola console. Because Casimir's was the only watering hole in Hamtramk with a television set in those days, the place was always packed on fight night (even though you had to be within two feet of the tiny screen to see anything at all). Nevertheless, the crowds came, and more often than not provided better fights than the ones being televised from Madison Square Garden, particularly after large amounts of hard-earned money changed hands over illegal (and ill-advised) boxing wagers. (It's rumored that more than one auto worker got his gizzard slit in the alley behind Casimir's over a welched bet, but I don't know that for a fact.)

It was a rough place, though, and Dagmar worried about Janos. She would sit up waiting every Friday evening well past midnight, until Janos would finally stagger home (smelling like a skunk) and pass out on the sofa. It was disgusting.

"A fine example you set for Lazlo," Dagmar would say to him the next day, waiting until his hangover reached its peak and every corpuscle in his throbbing head seemed ready to explode.

"Don't start with me, woman," he would moan. "Lazlo don't know nuttink."

"He knows more than you tink."

And she was right. Lazlo always knew when his father came home drunk. He wanted to know everything that was going on, so he would lie in his bed at night and pretend to sleep, his little spy's ear tuned to every sound in the house when one of his parents wasn't there. He pretended he was a ghost who could hear and not be heard, who could see and not be seen. He wondered why his father would want to go out every Friday night and make himself sick. It didn't make sense, even to a three-year-old.

It didn't make sense to Dagmar, either. After a few months she laid down the law.

"Either you are married to me or you are married to Casimir's bar. Which will it be?"

"Are you *threatenink* me?" Janos looked at her in disbelief; he had never heard her speak up for herself like this. What happened to the obedient elephant girl from the provinces? *She is truly becoming an American woman*, he thought. *What have I done?*

"If that is how you wish to put it," she said icily, handing him his coffee. She looked straight into his bloodshot eyes. She meant business, all right.

*Uh-oh,* thought Lazlo, who was spying from behind the bedroom door. *This could be serious! I could be an orphan any minute now!*

Janos considered the situation. Remember, Dagmar was still an exceptionally beautiful woman—tall and sinewy, with perfect breasts and a pout like Greta Garbo. She could have any man in Hamtramk (in all of Detroit, probably); they would *line up* just to kneel at her feet. He knew that. And he was short and homely, not exactly accustomed to beating women off with a stick. He knew that, too. It was no contest.

"You are right," he said. "I am married to you. And I have not been such a good husband."

"Oh, Janos!" she cried, relieved that he had given in, "You are a *wonderful* husband! You are best husband any woman could want!" Whereupon she picked him up and smothered him with wet kisses, just as she had done on their wedding night. Janos knew immediately that he had said exactly the right thing as he steered her into the bedroom.

He also saw the opening he needed. If he could make such a great sacrifice for his wife as to give up Friday nights at Casimir's, then she should be willing to indulge him in something *he* really wanted without complaining.

The next Monday he went to Grinnell's Department Store and, with a little more help from the Detroit Bank & Trust, bought a brand new fourteen-inch RCA console television set (better even than Casimir's Motorola) so that he could watch Friday Night Fights at home and save his marriage at the same time.

Lazlo didn't realize it then, but that day he became the first kid in Hamtramk to have a television set in his very own house, and his life would never be the same again.

# TEN

The genie was out of the bottle, all right, and he moved smack into the middle of the Horvath living room, commanding everyone's attention like Merlin the magician. The fourteen-inch black-and-white RCA console wasn't just a television set; it was a sacred shrine to the genie—a shining mahogany-veneered altar before which Janos, Dagmar and little Lazlo all gathered to watch the electronic wizard strut his stuff and celebrate their newly-achieved Americanhood— because in 1948 a television set was considered to be the ultimate status symbol, and owning one meant that Janos and Dagmar had finally arrived. They had not only "kept it up with the Jones family," they had done the Jones family one better.

The genie gave Janos everything he wanted. Now he could stay home and watch the fights, which not only made Dagmar happy, but also allowed Janos a few hours a week to gloat (privately, of course) about the fact that he had a television set at home and most of his buddies didn't, which made *him* happy. And because he owned a television set, he became very popular at the plant, cultivating a reputation as a very gracious host whose beautiful and devoted wife served up sausages and beer to the lucky few who were invited over on Friday nights to watch the "Gillette Cavalcade of Sports." It was all free, and everybody agreed that it sure beat the hell out of Casimir's Bar, where you could barely see the screen and patrons were often getting beaten up or killed over nothing at all.

Lazlo was allowed to stay up and watch the fights, too. (Many of Janos's friends from the plant were curious about this three-year-old boy who didn't talk; at first he was like a sideshow attraction in a traveling carnie—household visitors would look at him with the curiosity they usually reserved for people who bite the heads off chickens—then they would try tricks on him to make him speak, often betting among themselves on the results. But Lazlo wasn't stupid and he couldn't be tricked; he would speak when he was damn good and ready.)

"He don't talk yet," Janos would say, shrugging his shoulders as though embarrassed by Lazlo's silence. "I tink maybe he is just shy," and then the visitors would leave him alone and watch the fights.

Lazlo would prop himself up on the sofa next to his father and watch the genie in awe and wonderment. Sometimes it got a little rowdy at the Horvath household, with everybody yelling and swearing and shouting as two little guys on the television screen danced around punching each other out. Lazlo didn't get it. He couldn't understand why two people would want to beat each other up, or *be* beaten up, for that matter. It looked to him like it hurt. And especially he didn't understand why all these strange giants in his own living room would get so excited about somebody else getting his ass kicked. *They* weren't the ones getting their asses kicked! How would they like it if somebody hit *them* like that? He watched them all very carefully as they watched the television set, yelling and shouting every time anything happened. He was almost more interested in them than he was in what he was going on in that box.

There were some good prizefighters in those days: Sugar Ray Robinson, Willie Pep, Ezzard Charles, Jersey Joe Walcott, Kid Gavilan (with his famous bolo punch), Archie Moore, Joe Louis (the "Brown Bomber" from Detroit, who was by that time getting a little long in the tooth) and a new heavyweight, Rocky Marciano (the latest "Great White Hope" in the only sport of its time dominated entirely by black men). And Janos knew them all. At least he knew all *about* them, which made him feel like he knew them all personally, and he had memorized all of their statistics like it was Holy Scripture. His greatest pleasure in life was watching them beat the shit out of each other on his own television set—live from Madison Square Garden in New York City—while sitting in the comfort of his own living room, being waited on hand and foot by his dutiful and gracious wife, surrounded by his very best friends. What more could any man want? This was the promise of America come true!

But why did Lazlo choose to stay up late and watch two grown men pound each other into oblivion if he didn't like what he was seeing? Why didn't he just shuffle off to bed and let the adults behave like children without him (which they were going to do anyway)?

Because he couldn't, that's why. Because something had captured his little three-year-old imagination and wouldn't let go. Because he was seduced, hooked, addicted—*mesmerized*—from the very instant that the genie arrived on the scene, trapped inside an RCA fourteen-inch console television set. The genie (who could also disguise himself as a parrot on these occasions) sang to him between rounds, when the men weren't fighting:

"To *look* sharp, every time you shave,
To *feel* sharp, and be on the ball,
Just *be* sharp..." (Well, you know the rest.)

In any case, that's how Lazlo, at the age of three, first came to grips with his manhood and his destiny, knowing that if he used Gillette Blue Blades he would not only be sharp, he would always be happy. The genie had told him so, and there was no reason to doubt that it was true. After all, genies don't lie.

# ELEVEN

**W**e take too much for granted these days. Technology has become so sophisticated that sometimes we forget what it was like not so long ago when (God forbid!) we actually had to entertain ourselves. Now everything is done for us and we never have to leave home; all we have to do is push a button. We have wall-sized remote-control stereo television sets, compact discs, laser discs, VCRs, three networks, hundreds of syndicated stations and cable TV with 128 channels; we have computer games and Nintendo; we can sit in our living rooms and do our Christmas shopping, get psychiatric help, and watch our elected officials make fools of themselves; we have talking books and silent radio; we have news, weather and sports all day long; we have religious services and por-nographic movies; we have just about everything we could ever want now, all in exchange for one small thing: the vivid and unique imaginations we were all born with. Looking back, I think that must have been the deal we made with the

Devil just so that we could be entertained twenty-four hours a day.

Because it wasn't always like that. Television was very primitive in the early days, and very corny. Nothing was on at all until seven o'clock at night, and then the most revolutionary communications medium in the history of the world gave us such daring exotic programs as "Adventures of Okey Doky," "Face the Music," "Gay Nineties Revue" and (certainly my favorite) "Author Meets the Critics." The taste and intelligence of the American public was assaulted from day one, and there are those who say that not that much has changed over the years.

But there were some good programs, too. "Philco TV Playhouse" and "Texaco Star Theater" provided some interesting original drama, and Ed Sullivan's "Toast of the Town" gave us a chance to see entertainers we would never have seen otherwise, and some of them actually had talent. Good or bad, sophisticated or corny, Lazlo watched it all with equal interest. He decided that television would be his window to the world, no matter what he might see through that window. He didn't make judgments then and he doesn't make them now, which is one of the things I love about him.

Sometimes I see him sitting in that little house in Hamtramk as clearly as I see my own childhood. Having no brothers or sisters, no friends, unable to read, not yet ready to talk, consigned Monday through Friday to the inescapable custody of Mrs. Kluzewski (who, like a prison matron, spent most of her time ignoring him), Lazlo's days were endless, each one an eternity, as he waited for the television genie to reappear every night and ignite his three-year-old imagination like nothing ever had before, to sing him to sleep with his endless repertoire of happy little commercials, transporting him to a magical land where no one was ever lonely, a land beyond the all-too-familiar walls of his tiny room, beyond the park where all the other kids played but he couldn't, beyond the ugly, black, belching smokestacks of Hamtramk, beyond anything he had ever known or even thought to exist—a land where everything was always perfect, where everyone was always happy, where every dream came true: The land of television jingles.

Lazlo finally knew what he would be when he grew up: He would be a dreamer.

# TWELVE

**W**hy do we always seem to make fun of the dreamers while we marvel at the results of their dreams? I don't get it. ( I admit, some dreams are better than others, but we *all* have dreams, and I don't know anybody who makes fun of his *own* dreams, do you?) I mean, consider Edison and Einstein, Newton and Galileo, Jesus, Mohammed and Gandhi; Martin Luther King, William Shakespeare, Marie Curie, Michelangelo, Leonardo. This list goes on forever, and the one thing they all had in common was that they were all ridiculed for their dreams. Sometimes they were even killed for them. And just think where we'd be today without them and their "crazy" dreams.

Without dreams, Lazlo's parents never would have joined the circus, never would have met, never would have fallen in love, never would have had Lazlo, never would have come to America. In fact, without dreams, there never would have been an America for them to come to.

If it weren't for dreams there would be no radio, no television, no man would have ever set foot on the moon, and there certainly wouldn't be Tuesday Night Football.

That's why I never laughed at Lazlo for wanting to be a dreamer. It beats the hell out of wanting to be President, if you ask me.

# THIRTEEN

**O**n that fateful day when Lazlo finally decided to speak, it came as such a shock to his parents that they themselves became speechless. It wasn't necessarily the fact that it had taken Lazlo three years to utter so much as a single word, or even the fact that the very first thing that ever came out of his mouth (other than food, of course) happened to be a perfectly formed sentence. No. What stopped Dagmar and Janos in their tracks was what the boy actually *said*.

This (at least as I understand it) is what happened, and it may even be true:

It was a Sunday in August, hotter than the hubs of hell, and Janos was about to take the Family Horvath out for their weekly drive in the Studebaker. From the time Janos and the bank bought the car, it had become more or less of a tradition to get in it and go somewhere every Sunday. The Horvaths never planned their destination, and they never went to the same place twice, (Janos was one of those people who believe

41

that once you've seen something, you've really seen it; this attitude could have a devastating effect on someone's sex life, I suppose, but that's a whole other story.)

In any case, the Horvaths piled into the Studebaker that Sunday and set out for Belle Isle, a large, wooded park with picnic tables and teeter-totters and rowboats for rent; it was located in the middle of the Detroit River, closer to the Canadian side. You're probably thinking that this was a very boring place, and of course you're right.

But it wasn't boring to Lazlo. Nothing was, once he got out of the house and into the world. And Belle Isle park held a particular fascination for him because it was there that he saw in the flesh, for the first time in his young life, people who were a different color from him. Black people. Brown people. White giants who spoke Martian he was used to, for he lived in Hamtramk. And all the people on television, who spoke perfect English and always seemed to be happy, they were white, too. But here in this park were black giants who spoke English, along with their black children, a lot of them no bigger than Lazlo. He was so fascinated by the sight of them that he just stood and stared, wondering to himself why they were black and he wasn't. He though it might be fun to be black, but he never said that because up until this point in his life he still hadn't said anything.

His father noticed him staring at a black family with a look of bewilderment on his face and misunderstood it to be fear.

"Do not be afraid of them, Lazlo," he said. "They are just the same as us. Everybody is equal in USA. Everybody the same. That is what makes USA such a great country."

Of course it wasn't until much later that Lazlo found out that Janos's vision of racial equality in the Great American Melting Pot was more wishful thinking than reality, but his father's words nevertheless managed to take root in Lazlo's impressionable little mind and stay there forever. It was the greatest gift Janos could have ever given his son, because it can truly be said that from that moment on, Lazlo Horvath never judged another human being by the color of his skin. In fact, he never judged anybody at all. Whatever people were, they were. And it was all right with him. Sometimes in the days that followed he did wonder, though, why he never saw any black giants on television commercials. Didn't they deserve to be just as happy as everybody else?

That Sunday, as the Horvaths were about to leave for home, the Studebaker had other ideas. It decided to stay. Janos, who knew nothing about mechanical things despite the fact that he worked as a welder in an automobile plant (and was too proud to ask any stranger for help), opened the hood of the car and banged on the carburetor with a monkey wrench, as though that would magically get the old crate chugging again. But it was no use; when he turned the key, all he heard was the dying whir of a meatless meatgrinder. There they were, stranded in the Belle Isle parking lot as the Sunday sun dropped like a rock into the Detroit River.

"This fucking Studebaker," he muttered, his voice echoing the contempt he held for the Nazis and the Russians. It never occurred to him that the car might just be out of gas. Dagmar looked on helplessly, anticipating the long walk home.

From the back seat Lazlo looked out the window. He, too, knew nothing about cars or what made them go; he was only three and wasn't expected to know such things. A short distance away he saw a black family, happy and relaxed after a fine day at the park, get into their Chevy coupe and drive off. It was like watching a commercial.

"See the USA in a Chevrolet," he said in his little voice— a little voice his parents had never heard form actual words before, let alone a complete sentence.

It took several moments for the full impact of this historic event to hit them.

"Yah, yah," said Janos. "That is easy for *you* to say."

Then he realized what had happened, and his eyes bugged out as he turned to Dagmar, who was totally dumbfounded. Janos and Dagmar stared at each other in astonishment, completely forgetting their predicament. Simultaneously they turned to Lazlo, who was still wistfully gazing out the window.

"What did you say, Lazlo?" asked Janos very carefully, as though afraid of scaring the boy back into silence.

"See the USA in a Chevrolet," repeated Lazlo evenly, and he meant it.

"He talks!" gasped Dagmar, who was so stunned and happy that she burst out crying. "Janos, Lazlo can *talk*!"

"Our son is a genius! I knew it all along!" Janos shouted, deliriously pounding the steering wheel and laughing like a Magyar. He and Dagmar laughed and cried and hugged and kissed, while Lazlo sat in the back smiling because his parents were so happy.

All the way back to Hamtramk on the bus Lazlo never said another word, but it didn't matter. He had already spoken.

Janos, who had never before bragged about his son, told this story to everyone he knew, and even some people he didn't know so well. Now it may only be a coincidence, but "See the USA in your Chevrolet" later became a national campaign slogan for General Motors. Is it possible that Lazlo created one of the most successful advertising jingles of all time with the very first words out of his mouth, and didn't even know it? I wasn't there, so I can't say.

# FOURTEEN

Janos, who was once worried that Lazlo might be an idiot, was now convinced that the boy was brilliant. Of course, neither case was true, though it was interesting not only that Lazlo always spoke in complete sentences (usually quoting product slogans he had heard on the radio or television), but that there was never even a trace of an accent. "You'll wonder where the yellow went when you brush your teeth with Pepsodent," he would say, and his parents would laugh and applaud with pride and delight. Lazlo's little voice had the perfect mid-western American inflection that professional announcers and newscasters spend years trying to learn. It wasn't long before Janos and Dagmar were turning to their son for instruction in correct English pronunciation.

One Saturday morning, after a particularly serious night of drinking with his friends while watching the fights, Janos had such a hangover that you would have thought it had been *he* who had been in the ring getting his ears pounded. His temples throbbed, his eyeballs ached, and the icebag on his head was absolutely useless. All he could do was lie on his bed and moan like a wounded rhino. Lazlo heard this and, feeling concern for his father, tiptoed very quietly into the room and stood silently by the bed, a glass of water in his hand. He was sure, judging by the terrible sounds coming from his father, that Janos was about to croak any minute and, if he couldn't do anything to save his life, at least he didn't want to miss the event. He liked Janos, even though he thought he was kind of strange, and he didn't think it was fair that his father could actually die just from watching television and drinking too much beer.

"Go away, Lazlo," Janos groaned from under the blankets. "I don't feel so good today. Please go play in the traffic or sometink."

But Lazlo didn't budge.

"So now you don't listen to your papa no more, eh, Mister Smarty Alex? I'm in pain, Lazlo. I hurt really bad. Please fuck off."

Lazlo had no intention of fucking off. It was an expression he never heard on television, thus he had no idea what it meant. He stood his ground.

"For fast, fast, fast relief," he chirped, "try Speedy Alka-Seltzer."

"Uhhhh..." said Janos. His voice sounded like water running down a bathtub drain. The very last thing on earth he wanted to hear, with the possible exception of a train wreck outside the window, was an Alka-Seltzer commercial coming from the lips of his four-year-old son. But Lazlo, who was determined to make his father happy (or at least to keep him alive a while longer) took two little round Alka-Selzer tablets from his pocket and dropped them into the glass of water anyway. The water began to fizz, just like it did on television. Lazlo handed the glass to his father, who was getting so desperate that he would try anything—especially if it would get Lazlo out of the room.

Miraculously, within a few minutes Janos felt the pounding in his head stop, and soon he was standing under a hot shower, singing a romantic gypsy ballad in the vicinity of the key of D minor and vowing to himself never to drink again. Lazlo, he thought, is a truly gifted child. He might even have a future in medicine.

# FIFTEEN

**L**azlo had other ideas. Not that he had anything in particular against the medical profession, but he was the son of
circus performers. His parents were married in the circus; for
all he knew, he had even been *conceived* in the circus. Yes,
performing was in his blood, just as dreams were in his head.
It had now been two years since he had first talked; two years
of Howdy Doody, Buffalo Bob, Milton Berle, the Lone
Ranger, Soupy Sales, Kukla, Fran & Ollie, not to mention a
never-ending supply of wonderful commercials with happy
people and snappy jingles. Lazlo was a child of the future,
and the future was television.

One day, as Lazlo was walking with the dreaded Mrs.
Kluzewski to Wolski's Bakery on Caniff Road, he was lured by
the sweet, familiar aroma of the *herbatniki, ciastko* and *buleczki*
hot out of the oven; there was no need for Mrs. K to drag him
along by the arm, though that's what she did anyway. It was
her habit, ever since Dagmar told her that Lazlo was too big

for the stroller and perfectly capable of walking. Wafting out of the Polish-American Hall next door to the bakery, into the gray industrial smog of Hamtramk and the din of the mid-day traffic, was the unmistakable piston beat of Mirek Celinski and his Fabulous Polecats. Lazlo had never heard anything quite like it; the music resonated to the depths of his five-year-old soul. It was the call of an Old Country he had never known, the anthem of ancestors he was yet to discover. The bank was playing the "Hungarian Polka," and somehow he just had to hear it better.

Once inside the bakery, Mrs. Kluzewski ran into two of her cronies from the park and momentarily let go of Lazlo's hand to embrace her friends. The day's gossip was so juicy that Mrs. K completely immersed herself in this animated Martian conversation, forgetting that Lazlo was even there. And by the time she remembered and turned around, he wasn't.

He stood, unseen, just inside the doorway of the Polish-American Hall. A stoop-shouldered old man of at least ninety was mopping the floor, totally ignoring Mirek Celinski and his Fabulous Polecats, who were rehearsing for an upcoming engagement at the Westside Riverview Lanes Bowling Alley and Lounge. The old geezer may have heard it all a million times, but the quartet was playing with such style and authority that Lazlo was spellbound. The sounds they made filled him with a kind of joy he had never known before; it was thrilling beyond his wildest imagination. *This must be how all those happy people in the television commercials feel all the time,* he decided. It was a tingly sensation he couldn't put into words, except that he knew it was perfect.

Lazlo couldn't take his eyes off Mirek Celinski, whose fingers flew over the buttons and keys of the enormous accordion with dazzling speed. They seemed to have minds of their own, always producing the right notes at the right time, while Celinski (tall and silver-haired, as dashing a figure as

Lazlo had ever seen on television) swayed and smiled to the rhythm of the music, squeezing the bellows of the instrument, caressing it—fondling it—as though it were a woman. To the five-year-old boy hiding in the shadow of the doorway, Mirek Celinski looked like a Greek god, or at the very least a Polish prince.

But even princes, when they drink too much beer during rehearsals, have to pee. When the tune ended Mirek Celinski put down his accordion, lit a cigarette and told the Fabulous Polecats to "take five." One by one the others followed him off stage and disappeared into the men's room to relieve themselves. The old custodian finished mopping, picked up his pail and shuffled off into the kitchen. Lazlo was the only one left. The hall, without the music, was suddenly very quiet and a little spooky.

Lazlo barely heard the police siren outside, nor did he realize it was for him. It hadn't occurred to him that Mrs. Kluzewski (who was always in great fear of losing her job) would call the cops the minute she noticed him missing. Besides, even if it had occurred to him, he wouldn't have gone back. Not yet. Some things were more important than Mrs. K's paranoia.

The old Hohner accordion sat on stage like a gleaming idol, commanding Lazlo's inspection. Overcoming his fear of being discovered, he inched his way toward the bandstand to get a closer look at this magnificent instrument.

To Lazlo it was a big as a refrigerator, a huge, beautiful, baffling box with real ivory keys (Lazlo didn't know anything about the shameful elephant poaching in those days; if he had he would have been very upset) and ebony buttons. The casing was carefully inlaid with gold filigree, and on the sides and back were painted pictures of pastoral scenes of life in a typically quaint Polish village. (*It was not only a musical instrument*, he thought, *but a work of art!*) But how did it work? How could such wonderful sounds come out of this contraption, and who in the world was clever enough to decipher all those buttons and keys? Mirek Celinski, that's who. *I was right,* Lazlo decided. *Mirek Celinski is God. No mortal human being could make this thing work.* Lazlo ran his hand ever-so-lightly across every feature of the accordion, reverently, as though trying to understand its magical powers by touch. To his dismay the damn thing just sat there, making no sound whatsoever.

Urged on by his boyish curiosity, Lazlo stepped up on stage and, looking around to make sure no one was watching, picked up the gigantic squeezebox. It wasn't as heavy as he thought it would be, though it was nearly as big as he was, and he was already pretty big for a five-year-old. He slipped the leather straps over his shoulders and struck a pose, trying to remember every detail of what he had just seen and heard Mirek Celinski do. Gently he squeezed the box, and to his amazement a sound actually came out. Then he pulled his hands apart, and an altogether different sound came out. *This is fantastic!* he thought. *It's just like breathing, only when it breathes it makes music!* He tried it again, this time depressing some of the keys on one side and some of the buttons on the other; it made different sounds, all of them sweet. *This isn't so hard after all,* he decided.

He remembered (don't ask me how) the exact melody of the "Hungarian Polka" that Mirek and the Fabulous Polecats had just played, and he tried to find that same music on those keys and buttons. Note by note he picked it out, slowly at first, but perfectly, and it made him very happy.

I wasn't there, of course, but Mirek Celinski told me this story personally, so I have every reason to believe that it's true. Mirek and the other guys were still in the john, pissing like racehorses and arguing about an augmented seventh, when they heard some strange noises coming from inside the hall. They suddenly fell silent, for they knew there was no one in the place except themselves and the old geezer, and

the only thing *he* played was a mop. No, there was definitely
something weird going on, but nobody wanted to be the first
to investigate, for Mirek (like all the other Polecats) was
deeply superstitious. But the music continued, and it had a
lightness and purity to it that was almost angelic. "Holy shit,"
said Mirek, "it's the 'Hungarian Polka'!" and the others
agreed. Finally he made the sign of the cross and bravely
stuck his head outside the men's room door.

There, on the bandstand, was a chubby little boy playing
an accordion roughly his size, and playing it as though he had
played it from birth. In the space of less than five minutes,
Lazlo had mastered a very difficult tune he had never heard
before on an impossible instrument he had never even *seen*
before, and he was having the time of his life.

Mirek Celinski stormed out of the lavatory, followed by
his Polecats.

"Who the devil do you think you are?!" he shouted,
trying to control his anger and humiliation. "And what the
devil do you think you're doing?"

Lazlo stopped playing. He was embarrassed about being
caught red-handed. All he wanted to do was run. In an
instant he had forgotten how much fun he'd been having.
Then he remembered. A big smile crossed his face.

"I'm Lazlo," he said. "I can make music happen."

# SIXTEEN

**W**here does the time go, when it goes?

Do people get cancer all of a sudden, or do they have to work at it for a long time?

Why does music sound better in harmony than in unison?

Lazlo, the child, wanted answers to these questions, and many others. I don't know if he ever found them. I think he probably did. Maybe he knew all along.

He certainly knew how to play the accordion. Mirek Celinski saw to that. The *Polkameister* himself was so impressed by Lazlo's uncanny ability that day in the Polish-American Hall that he took the boy under his wing and taught him every song he knew. It didn't take long, because once Lazlo heard a tune he could play it back perfectly. Everyone who saw and heard it was amazed. And Mirek Celinski, far from being threatened by the talent of his little protégé, couldn't have been more proud. After all, wasn't it he who had discovered Lazlo in the first place? Mirek may have been corny, but he was no fool. Running into Lazlo was like finding the Hope Diamond in a coal bin. Now he had someone he could pass his rich musical legacy on to, as he would to his son if he had had a son. Not that that was his only interest. *Nuts to those clowns in the band,* thought Mirek, *I've got a fat little Mozart on my hands! What a find! What a gimmick!* Mirek Celinski was so convinced that Lazlo was his ticket to fame at last that he actually gave the boy his prized 1872 rosewood *Soprani* accordion, one of several near-priceless instruments in his vast squeezebox collection.

Janos and Dagmar, of course, were just as astonished as everyone else. Neither of them could carry a tune in a bushel basket, and here was their offspring playing all of Brahms's Hungarian Dances (not to mention 247 different polkas) by ear! He was a midget virtuoso! Deeply superstitious people, Janos and Dagmar were now certain that their son had been touched by the hand of God, and they had no intention of messing with any fate as heavy as that. What were they supposed to do—defy the Almighty and forbid Lazlo to play with the band? Deny the boy his destiny? Not a chance. So, at the ripe old age of five, Lazlo became a featured performer with Mirek Celinski and his Fabulous Polecats, but only on weekends and only for the first set, because the second set was way past his bedtime.

Lazlo's first gig with the Polecats was a Friday night at the Westside Riverview Lanes Bowling Alley and Lounge (*"AMF Automatic Pinspotters, Fifty Lanes, No Waiting, Leagues Welcome"*), and it was there that he met the woman of his dreams. But we'll get to that later....

Even now I have to laugh when I imagine little Lazlo perched on top of the bar near the bandstand (he was so short that he could only be seen if he stood on the bar), strapped into his oversized squeezebox, doing a kind of "duelling accordions" with his new friend and teacher, Mirek Celinski. Naturally the crowd loved it, and this wasn't a crowd that loved much of anything. Their lousy jobs at the Dodge Main plant across the street didn't exactly make them the easiest audience in the world to entertain. But who could resist Lazlo, standing up there squeezing and grinning, thrilled to death just to be making all these miserable people so happy with his music?

Once the word spread that Lazlo was playing, the curious came from all over town. The bar was jammed; the bowlers stopped bowling, the eaters stopped eating, the lovers stopped...well, you know. It seemed like all of Hamtramk showed up at the Westside Riverview Lanes for Lazlo's debut. And they weren't disappointed. The kid was sensational.

So was Wanda Pozniak. And she didn't even play the accordion. She didn't have to; all Wanda had to do was stand behind the bar in her pink pedal pushers and Playtex bra (the real pointy kind that was popular in those days) under a fuzzy white angora sweater, serving up drinks to the factory workers while Lazlo, Mirek and all the Fabulous Polecats played their asses off.

Standing there on the bar, looking down at those perfectly-shaped breasts, Lazlo fell in love. Wanda was twenty-six and she'd been around the block. A campaign-hardened veteran of a brief stint on the women's pro bowlers' tour and an even briefer marriage to Stan Pozniak, a boorish lout who couldn't stand the fact that his wife carried a higher bowling average than he did, she was tougher than a two-dollar steak. She wasn't what you'd call beautiful (like Dagmar was beautiful), but her body was nothing short of spectacular. Lazlo *wanted* that body, though he didn't have the faintest idea what he would do with it if he got it. It didn't matter. Wanda was perfection—the ideal woman—and every song Lazlo played he played just for her.

Whenever he caught her eye she was smiling up at him, and he knew that she wanted him, too. So what if she was old enough to be his mother? She'd just have to wait.

# SEVENTEEN

**B**ut Wanda was not about to wait. Not for Lazlo, anyway. One night, between songs, Lazlo gathered up all his courage, leaned over to Wanda and whispered, "I love you, Wanda." And Wanda, who was poured into the tightest, most provocative Capri pants you ever saw, looked up at him, clicked her Beeman's Blackjack gum, smiled and said, "Why, Lazlo, you're so sweet! If I ever have a little boy, I hope he's just like you."

Lazlo was devastated. He may have been only five but he wasn't stupid. All of a sudden he realized that Wanda didn't want him at all—she only thought of him as just another nice little kid who happened to be a virtuoso on the accordion. He was too young for her! (It's not the first time that age has got in the way of the course of True Love, but the effect on Lazlo was something he would surely never forget, for Wanda was perfect and she was forever unattainable.) Lazlo decided that he could never be satisfied with any woman who didn't measure up to the wonderfulness of Wanda, and what woman ever could? He saw a bleak future for himself in the romance department. First Love is a terrible burden for anyone to carry, let alone a five-year-old, but then Lazlo was no ordinary five-year-old.

He *was* Lazlo, though, and he could make music happen. What's love, after all, compared to music? *Well*, Lazlo figured, *when you're five and you've found one of the two, that's better than nothing*. As painful as it was, he knew he'd just have to forget Wanda and get on with his task of making people happy.

And he did. As the weeks went by, they couldn't handle the Friday night throngs at the Westside Riverview Lanes Bowling Alley and Lounge. Sure, there were still the fifty lanes and AMF automatic pinspotters, but nobody used them anymore. They all came to see Lazlo. The bar was doing great business, but the bowling alley was going broke.

So it was that Stanley Pozniak, the owner and manager of the Westside Riverview Lanes Bowling Alley and Lounge (and former husband of the voluptuous Wanda), decided to replace Mirek Celinski and his Fabulous Polecats Featuring Lazlo, "The Hungarian Mozart of Hamtramk." Stanley didn't like the idea of losing money. He also didn't much care for polka music. And he particularly didn't like the way Lazlo looked at Wanda whenever he played a gypsy love song (it takes a very strange man to be insanely jealous of a pudgy five-year-old boy, but that was Stanley). In short, he cancelled the gig.

Mirek Celinski wasn't concerned. He didn't need Stanley, he didn't need the Westside Riverview Lanes Bowling Alley and Lounge, he didn't need anything; he had Lazlo—his ticket to the Big Time. He told Stanley in plain Polish what he could do with his bowling alley and lounge (*and* his AMF automatic pinspotters) and immediately booked the act into the Grosse Pointe Yacht Club.

While the patrons of the Westside Riverview Lanes were being treated to the insipid background noise of Roman Berenski's "talking piano," Lazlo's name was becoming a household word all over Detroit. His reputation even reached the ears of several local talent scouts (who, as we all know, are usually the last people on God's green earth to recognize talent). And while dollar signs danced like sugar plums in the minds of Mirek Celinski and every one of his Fabulous Polecats, Janos and Dagmar were preparing Lazlo for entry into kindergarten.

Mirek and the Fabulous Polecats rehearsed. Lazlo didn't have to. He had already heard the music once. But Janos and Dagmar spent the week trying to familiarize him with the alphabet. It was not an easy task, since neither of them was very clear on how many letters there actually were in English, let alone what those letters sounded like or meant. (I'm happy to report that for Lazlo it was all very clear on the first day of school because Janina Vitry, a classmate to whom he would always be grateful, had gone to a YWCA summer camp on Belle Isle and learned to sing the alphabet like all the English-speaking kids did. Lazlo heard it once and added it immediately to his repertoire.)

Friday was a momentous day. Janos and Dagmar took Lazlo to the Grosse Pointe Yacht Club instead of the Westside Riverview Lanes. He knew immediately he would never see Wanda again, and there was a bittersweet sound to his accordion that night. Then, between sets, when Lazlo was finished playing, all those who had dollar-sign dreams converged backstage and the real trouble began. In any language, it became clear to Lazlo that the Fabulous Polecats thought it would be just fine to change their name from "Mirek Cilenski and the Fabulous Polecats" to "Lazlo Horvath and the Fabulous Polecats," dropping Mirek altogether. Lazlo could also tell that Mirek, his hero, the man who had given him one of the finest accordions ever made, would gladly sacrifice his Polecats and break away to start a new career with Lazlo as a duo, even taking second billing. The recording executives wanted to use Lazlo's age to sell records, and one New York booking agent wanted Lazlo alone—without Mirek *or* the Polecats—to appear on the Arthur Godfrey show and become "a child sensation."

Though Lazlo wanted to appear on television almost more than anything in the world, he knew it was a rotten deal. He couldn't do something like that to Mirek; it would break his heart. He couldn't even do that to the Polecats. He couldn't do that to anybody, because he wasn't equipped to hurt people. So he quit the band.

No amount of pleading would make him change his mind. He had begun to play music because he wanted to make people happy. Now they weren't happy. In fact, they were miserable—all on account of him. So he quit. No more Hungarian Rhapsodies. No more polkas. His first exposure to music had been his beloved jingles on the radio, and later on the genie called television. He decided he would stick to jingles, because jingles made everybody happy.

The commotion eventually died down when everyone saw that Lazlo meant what he said; he was finished with the band. He even tried to give Mirek his accordion back, but Mirek wouldn't take it. A deal was a deal, a gift was a gift. Mirek was frustrated but loved Lazlo for sticking up for his convictions. The Polecats broke up, but Mirek put together a new group in Eau Claire, Wisconsin, and played at the Pizza & Polka Palace until he retired more than twenty years later. I think one of his prized Hohners is now on display at the Smithsonian Institution in Washington, D.C., but I'm not sure.

Lazlo went on to kindergarten and his pursuit of happiness. He played small accordion parts in school plays, as requested, and spent his evenings watching television. He liked that best of all.

# EIGHTEEN

Lazlo's childhood became as normal as that of any Hungarian kid raised in a Polish neighborhood in America. He stuck mostly to himself. He learned how to read because he had to for school, but it never really appealed to him. Fortunately there were no books in the house. He turned to the television genie for his refuge and his entertainment, and happiness bubbled in him just as it did in the heroes and heroines of the cathode ray tube. Lazlo didn't dance to the beat of a different drummer; he danced to the beat of the television commercial. His tempo was the tempo of the sixty-second spot. Life was good, and getting better all the time. He had already learned all he would ever need to know to be happy.

Meanwhile, Janos was growing more and more disenchanted with his welding job at Dodge Main. The Horvaths were comfortable enough, but the auto plant was a dead end for an ambitious man like Janos. And he particularly didn't like the fact that the only way they could "keep it up with the Jones family" was by Dagmar stuffing sausages eight hours a day at the Kowalski factory. Her hands were starting to look a little rough, and her disposition wasn't so great, either. No longer was she the submissive elephant girl from Hungary who let him get away with murder and told him how wonderful he was. She really was becoming (God forbid!) an American woman. As far as Janos was concerned, it wasn't a change for the good. There had to be a better way of life.

So in June of Lazlo's thirteenth year, despite the fears of Dagmar and the warnings of Janos's friends (who would hate to see the end of the free Friday night television parties), Janos packed up their most precious belongings, lashed the television set and his favorite chair to the top of the old Studebaker, took his life savings, his vacation pay and the latest copy of *TV Guide,* put Dagmar and Lazlo in the car and set out for California.

They never got there.

# NINETEEN

The Studebaker finally gave up the ghost on a two-lane blacktop highway somewhere outside of Tucson, right between Burma Shave signs.

"You miserable bucket of bolts! This time I kill you, I promise!" bellowed Janos, kicking the fender with his Florsheims as Dagmar tried in vain to hush him (she didn't want Lazlo to hear his father talk about killing anything). But the old crate was already dead and no amount of kicking or cursing could change that, any more than all the hopes and prayers in the world could join Lazlo with his beloved Wanda, who had long since given up bowling and begun a new career as the devoted wife of a Detroit frozen food distributor.

The Family Horvath had no choice but to get out and walk, carrying as many of their belongings as they could manage. Lazlo, who was by now bigger than both his parents, carried most of the stuff, including his accordion case. The three of them looked like beasts of burden as they trudged along the scorching desert road, but Lazlo didn't mind at all. He was anxious to see and commit to memory all the Burma Shave signs.

Eventually they came to a one-pump gas station and ratty little diner at a dusty crossroads in the middle of nowhere. Nowhere, Arizona. Population 6.

Janos was very discouraged. The dream of California seemed to have died along with the Studebaker, and never, not even when they were fleeing Hungary so many years ago, did he feel more like a refugee than he did at that very moment. The apparent hopelessness of the situation took its toll on Janos, and Lazlo was worried that his father would just surrender to this little run of bad luck. Never had he seen him so unhappy. Janos seemed to grow old before the boy's very eyes.

Looking up, Lazlo noticed a big red Texaco sign above the gas station, and he was suddenly relieved.

"Don't be sad, Pop," he said cheerfully. "You can trust your car to the man who wears the star."

Janos looked at his overgrown son like he wanted to smack him, but of course Lazlo was too big (and too nice) to smack. That didn't stop Janos from wanting to, though.

"Maybe the man who wears the star would like to adopt my idiot son," Janos grumbled.

"Now, now," scolded Dagmar, "Lazlo don't mean any harm. He just wants you to see the good side of tings." Lazlo nodded in agreement. But looking around, all Janos could see beyond the gas station and diner were giant cactus plants, tumbling tumbleweed and boulders. Lots of boulders. His heart sank even lower.

Lazlo looked around at the very same scenery and saw something entirely different. (Lazlo always had a knack for seeing things a little differently than most people.) What he saw was a magnificent painted landscape of desert and mountains, the great American frontier unspoiled by people and cars and pollution (yes, kids, there was pollution even in those days; plenty of it). Most of all, what he saw reminded him of all the old cowboy movies he was used to watching on television.

"I like it here, Pop," he said. "Can we stay?"

"Over my dead body," replied Janos, who was on his way to California, with or without Lazlo.

# TWENTY

The Texaco man was a tribute to the star he wore on his hat. His name was Burleigh Drummond and he had lived in Nowhere all his life, twenty-eight years of it with his wife, Minnie. Together they ran the filling station and the diner, feeding, gassing, watering and oiling every stray motorist who occasionally happened by. They couldn't have been more hospitable; ever since the Interstate to Tucson put Nowhere off the map, very few people stopped to gas up anymore, and even fewer sampled Minnie's once-famous chicken fried steak. Sometimes it got kind of lonely in Nowhere.

"I guess I just like people," said Burleigh after telling the Horvaths his entire life story. "Sometimes I miss 'em."

"Then how come you still live in the middle of Nowhere?" Lazlo asked him.

"Because I don't like 'em all *that* much," Burleigh replied. "Sometimes I feel like selling the whole kit and kaboodle and moving to Barbados." Janos, though he had never heard of Barbados, conceded that the man had a point.

While Burleigh went to retrieve the Studebaker with his tow truck, Janos started thinking: What if Lazlo was right about something for a change? What if they *did* stay? What if *he* bought the diner and Texaco station? After all, he had some money saved up, and with his good credit all these years the bank was sure to give him a loan.

"Janos, you're crazy," said Dagmar.

"It was your son's idea," Janos said, passing the buck to Lazlo.

"Then he's crazy, too. You're both crazy. This place is Nowhere!"

"Not for long," whispered Janos. "Listen, I have a plan. I have a *vision*. Trust me."

So trust him she did. What choice did she have? (Women didn't have much of a voice in those days.) Still, she thought he was nuts.

Janos might have been many things, but he wasn't nuts. He really did have a vision: There were too many people on this planet, too many people in Tucson, and eventually most of them were going to have to have somewhere to go. Nowhere was only forty-five miles from the city, a straight shot with no traffic. And Tucson, like every other city, *had* to expand. When it did, the people certainly wouldn't want to live like prairie dogs in the desert. Nosiree, Bob; when they came to live in Nowhere they (being sophisticated Americans) would demand some sort of convenience for the very inconvenience of having to commute to the city from Nowhere every day.

What Janos envisioned was a combined little retail area that would provide everything that every future suburban commuter would ever want or need—a common marketplace to suit everyone's taste, open seven days a week, a restaurant, motel, gas station, department store, clothing shops, book store, movie theater, novelty shops, swimming pool, ice-skating rink and miniature golf course, all in one.

He would call it the Desert Mall. Sooner or later they would all come to him. He had thought of a better mousetrap, and the American Dream was suddenly within his grasp. He just *knew* it.

# TWENTY-ONE

The only other residents of Nowhere were Tom Crazy Fox, his wife Winona, and their two children, Walter and Gloria. They were Yuma Indians who lived in a 1948 Airstream trailer and sold hand-woven blankets, rattlesnake hides, ceremonial peace pipes and headdresses (made in Japan), and other souvenirs from a roadside shack. Business wasn't so good for them, either, ever since the Interstate bypassed Nowhere altogether. They were nice enough people, though, who kept to themselves and seemed to like living in Nowhere just fine.

But Minnie Drummond, who was getting on in years and had never been anywhere, wanted to leave. Nowhere was a drag. So when Janos suggested that he might be interested in buying the business if the price was right (Janos considered himself pretty cagey), Minnie jumped at the chance. Burleigh, now that Janos had called his bluff, suddenly wasn't so sure that he really wanted to sell, but Minnie gently told him that if he didn't she would cut him up into very small pieces and feed him to the coyotes. How often in a lifetime does a sucker like Janos stumble (literally) into the middle of Nowhere? Persuaded by Minnie's logic, Burleigh reluctantly agreed to sell the whole ball of wax for the bargain basement price of ten thousand dollars, which was every penny Janos could scrape up.

Convinced that they had pulled off the deal of the century, Minnie and Burleigh packed their belongings and hit the road for Barbados. And Janos, equally convinced that he had got the best of the deal and was well on his way to becoming a tycoon, was happier than Lazlo had ever seen him, even though Dagmar was so pissed off that she stopped talking to him for a whole month.

But for once in his life Janos had done something right. His years of experience with the Studebaker had made him into a serviceable mechanic, and word got around. Before long people were driving thirty or forty miles just to have him work on their cars. And while they waited, they would try some of Dagmar's homemade Hungarian goulash, which soon became as legendary as her beauty. Business boomed. Janos built a house on the property so that they wouldn't have to live in the back of the diner. He bought a brand new *color* RCA twenty-one-inch console television set and erected a fifty-foot antenna that could pull in a sharp picture all the way from Tucson. (I'm sure I don't have to tell you that this made Lazlo very happy.) Eventually Janos added two more gas pumps and another service bay, and had so much business that he had to hire Tom Crazy Fox to help out.

Lazlo, meanwhile, went to school in the nearest town, twenty-eight miles away. A school bus came for him every day, and he was its only passenger. He didn't mind because it gave him a chance to talk to the bus driver, who would challenge Lazlo's knowledge of jingles. It was a game; the bus driver would name a product and Lazlo would sing or play the jingle on his accordion. This went on every school day for years, and as far as I know the bus driver was never able to stump Lazlo.

Little by little Janos bought property like it was going out of style. And, just as he'd predicted, the people began moving away from the city to the middle of Nowhere, building houses, condos and an eighteen-hole championship golf course. Suddenly Nowhere was on the map, a bustling suburb teeming with yuppies (although they weren't called yuppies in those days) who did all their shopping at Janos Horvath's Desert Mall, which quickly appeared high on the list of *Fortune*'s corporations to watch. Janos had made his dream come true.

Not content with his incredible success (for true visionaries are never content), Janos came up with an even better idea: How about *mini-malls* in every neighborhood in every city in America? And if you think Janos was crazy then, just look around now.

Dagmar had no difficulty at all adjusting to a new life of untold wealth. She was able to stop working and devote all of her time to maintaining her legendary beauty, becoming the *Grande Dame* of the Desert, and one of the most popular social figures in all of Arizona. A rumor spread that she was really a Hungarian princess in exile, and if it wasn't Dagmar herself who started the rumor, at least she did nothing to stop it.

As for Lazlo, he had no delusions of grandeur, no lust for wealth. Money was nice, sure, but he could take it or leave it. He had a dream of his own, just like his father before him. He knew what he had to do: Make people happy. So at the age of eighteen he kissed Janos and Dagmar goodbye, packed up his accordion, and set out across America to become an ambassador of happiness—the King of the Jingles.

# PART TWO

# Lazlo the Jingle King

# ONE

**S**ometimes the distinction between dreams and reality gets a little blurry. Especially in Lazlo's case. And I'm not so sure it's such a bad thing. As long as Lazlo was happy (which he was), who was I to tell him that the circus going on in his mind wasn't really real? Maybe it was. It certainly was for *him*, so that's good enough for me.

If you've ever stayed in a Holiday Inn anywhere in North America, chances are good that you might have seen Lazlo in person. From the day he left home with his Samsonite suitcase and *Soprani* accordion, Lazlo did nothing but travel far and wide on his mission to make people happy by playing their favorite jingles, usually in the lounges of Holiday Inns. (I can't be sure of this, but I've heard that the term "happy hour" was first coined in the lounge of the Holiday Inn in Duluth, Minnesota, as Lazlo was playing there one afternoon; apparently a Great Lakes merchant seaman well known for his cynicism came into the bar and, seeing everybody laughing and singing and generally being happy, said, "What is this, the fuckin' happy hour?" and from then on that's what they called it.)

Lazlo played everywhere. Over the years there have been more confirmed Lazlo sightings in this country than all the Elvis and UFO sightings combined. He became famous— legendary, almost—without ever letting it go to his head. He never forgot that he was Lazlo, a simple Hungarian immigrant whose job it was to be happy and to make others happy with his jingles. His life never became complicated because he never tried to be anybody but Lazlo, and he didn't know how to tell a lie.

Every once in a while Lazlo would make his way back to Arizona to see his family and, most of all, his dear friend and spiritual adviser, Simon Blackthorn, a wise old Apache chief who lived in a tiny Indian village about two hundred miles from Nowhere. He had first met Simon at the Tulsa Holiday Inn in 1974 when Simon was in town trying to buy Shell Oil. (Simon was one rich Apache ever since the day he discovered a six-million-barrel-well of crude oil under his tepee after the government forced him and his people off their land and relocated them on a barren, completely useless patch of Arizona desert; Simon had the last laugh, and you can bet your Luchese boots that heads rolled at the Department of the Interior.)

Simon wasn't able to buy Shell Oil, but meeting Lazlo was almost as good. Simon liked Lazlo immediately. Lazlo reminded him of a 250-pound papoose with a kind of inner peace that he had rarely seen in any human being, white *or* red. He made Lazlo an honorary Apache right there at the Holiday Inn, and they have remained the best of friends to this very day.

# TWO

It was not a happy occasion that brought Simon and Lazlo together this time.

They sat in Simon's tepee, silently facing each other across a wooden table, passing a ceremonial peace pipe back and forth. It was dawn, and they had been that way all night, just sitting and smoking. With each puff of ceremonial smoke the silence grew more profound. Whatever was in that pipe made them both *very* mellow, which, come to think of it, is probably why it's called a "peace pipe."

Lazlo was the first to break the silence. He spoke slowly and quietly in the deliberate cadence of a spiritual pilgrim who had finally discovered some elusive universal truth.

"You only go 'round once in life, Simon," he said very solemnly. He was thinking about his boyhood friend, Wojciech, who had gone 'round once and recently checked out. That's right; Doctor Cool was history. Mr. Butts finally got

75

him. But he remained cool to the end, or at least that's what Lazlo heard.

"Be all that you can be," he continued with great sincerity. "Go for the gusto. Reach out and touch someone. Leave the driving to us. Pearls of wisdom, my friend."

"We've been down many trails together, Lazlo," said the old Indian, "and I've welcomed you into my lodge as a brother, but sometimes you're completely full of shit. Your friend from childhood dies of cancer and you eulogize him with *advertising* slogans? You can't do that!"

"I can't?" Lazlo demanded in all seriousness. "Why not?"

"Because life is extremely complicated and fragile," said Simon, who hated it when he was expected to be philosophical. "It's a miserable, temporary condition fraught with uncertainty and disappointment—a search for truth never to be found, an eternal quest for happiness denied to mortal men. Face it, Lazlo, life's a bitch."

"Not to *me* it isn't!" Lazlo protested, and he meant it. Life, to Lazlo, was anything *but* a bitch.

"That's because your daddy's rich and your mama's good-looking," said Simon. Then, catching himself: "Listen to me; I'm even starting to talk like you."

But Lazlo wasn't really listening to him. "You know what Wojciech's favorite jingle was, Simon?"

Simon didn't know. Simon didn't care.

"Chiquita Banana," said Lazlo wistfully. "Wojciech was crazy about Chiquita Banana." Softly, slowly, he started to sing the Chiquita Banana jingle, a tribute to his departed friend who had taught him that he didn't have to be cool:


"Hello, Amigos...
I'm Chiquita Banana and I've come to say,
Bananas have to ripen in a certain way;
When they're flecked with brown and have a golden hue

Bananas taste the best and are the best for you;
You can put them in a salad,
You can put them in a pie-ay,
Any way you want to eat them,
It's impossible to beat them.
But bananas like the climate of the
very, very tropical equator,
So you should never put bananas
In the refrigerator."

"That's good advice," said Simon, "but I don't think your friend Wojciech has to worry about it. He's probably in a refrigerator himself."

"I'm going to miss him, Simon."

"How long since you've seen him?"

"Thirty years," said Lazlo.

"Then another thirty or forty years shouldn't make that much of a difference," said Simon, who was not overly sentimental about life, death or anything. "You can always catch up with him in the happy hunting ground. Then you can fill him in on all the jingles he missed. Try not to be too broken-up about it."

"I'll be okay," said Lazlo. "You know me."

Simon nodded. He knew Lazlo, all right.

"Losing Wojciech is a very sad thing," Lazlo continued, "but it proves something I've said all along."

"And what might that be?" asked Simon, who didn't really want to know.

Lazlo broke into song: "I'm a pepper/You're a pepper..."

What the *hell* are you talking about?" demanded the Indian, who didn't watch much television and was woefully unfamiliar with the Dr. Pepper jingle.

"You gotta be a pepper, Simon!" said Lazlo, suddenly recovering from his melancholy. "You gotta get more cluck for your buck! Your gotta *live* while you're alive! You gotta *believe* in something! You gotta *dream!* You gotta find the *magic* in life! You can't just sit around the wigwam and get stoned all day."

"Lazlo, you find the magic in life your way, I'll find it my way," replied Simon, who didn't like being lectured in slogans, even by his best friend. "I'm a very simple man with very simple pleasures." (This was an ironic thing for Simon to say, considering the fact that his tepee was the command center for all of his various multinational business enterprises and looked more like the war room of the Pentagon than an Apache lodge. Side by side to the ancient tribal artifacts were computers, color monitors, telephones, a laser printer, a fax machine, ticker tape machines with direct lines to the stock exchanges in New York, London and Tokyo. Except for the Xerox color copier, the place could have been an AT&T showroom caught in a time warp. A simple man, indeed!)

"Still," Simon continued, not wishing to be too hard on his friend, "it's a wise man who listens to his heart. I think maybe you're a wise man, Lazlo, in a dumbass sort of way."

Lazlo was so moved by this expression of approval that he stood up, all 250 pounds of him in buckskin Indian garb, and embraced Simon in a great bear hug, lifting the old man right out of his chair.

"You're a true friend, Simon," he said, "and a faithful Indian companion."

# THREE

The phone rang and Lazlo released Simon from his grasp, just in time to prevent serious injury. (Lazlo, like a lot of very big men, didn't always know his own strength. I encountered quite a few very big men during my football career, but they, unlike Lazlo, were usually trying to hurt people, not necessarily make them happy.)

The call was for Lazlo.

"How did anybody know I was here?" asked Lazlo as Simon handed him the cordless AT&T Slimline phone. "Who is it?"

"It's Phineas Higgins," said Simon matter-of-factly. Lazlo went ashen.

In case you don't know it already, Phineas Higgins happens to be the richest man in the world, the president and CEO of Everything, Inc., the biggest, most powerful multinational conglomerate on the face of the earth. I'm not absolutely sure of this, but I don't think it's possible to buy any kind of product or use any kind of service anywhere on this planet without somehow contributing to the coffers of Everything, Inc.

Not that Lazlo was impressed by money (I've already told you that he could take it or leave it). After all, his father had money—tons of it. Simon Blackthorn had money. David Rockefeller had money. Donald Trump had money. But Phineas Higgins had MONEY, probably enough to pay off the national debt, and the power to go with it.

Not that Lazlo was impressed by power, either. In his lifetime he had seen too much of what power can do to people, and had long ago concluded that power isn't necessarily always such a good thing.

Phineas Higgins got right to the point (really powerful people *always* seem to get right to the point, which is often why they are mistakenly thought to be rude when they are just being powerful and efficient). Higgins informed Lazlo that he had seen him perform at the Skowhegan Holiday Inn and had decided right then and there that Lazlo Horvath was just the man he needed.

"Needed for what?" asked Lazlo, still a little stunned by the phone call.

"To get to Chicago on the next plane," said Higgins, as though the answer was self-evident.

It wasn't to Lazlo. "Why Chicago?" he asked, trying not to appear stupid.

"To save Tuesday Night Football," said Higgins gravely. "That doesn't make you nervous, does it?"

"No," said Lazlo. "Not if it'll make people happy."

"Nothing would make people happier," said Phineas Higgins. "They'll be delirious. I *sponsor* that show, and the ratings are abysmal. And do you know why? Because the viewers aren't happy, that's why. And when they're not happy they don't watch Tuesday Night Football, they watch home videos and cable."

"That's terrible," said Lazlo. "There aren't any commercials on cable and home video.

"Precisely. And when people don't see commercials, they don't buy. And when they don't buy, it makes *me* very unhappy."

"I'm sorry to hear that," said Lazlo, and he really was. "Why aren't they happy?"

"Because Tuesday Night Football's *boring*, that's why. It's stale. Ten years of the same lousy teams, the same dull games, the same stupid production. We're talking about CBA here, Lazlo, not ABC. Over at ABC they have all the legends of sports broadcasting—Gifford, Cosell, Meredith, Michaels— even Alex Karras, for pity's sake. Who've *we* got? Lance Allgood and Haywood Grueller!"

"Yes, I see what you mean," said Lazlo thoughtfully.

"There's no *chemistry* in the booth. People are turning their sets off in droves, and we've got to do something about it. We have to make them *happy* again. I'm counting on you to save Tuesday Night Football, Lazlo, or I'm afraid I'm going to have to pull the plug."

"Don't worry, Mr. Higgins," said Lazlo. "When you say Budweiser you've said it all. I won't let you down." But Higgins had already hung up; he knew that Lazlo wouldn't let him down before he ever even called. You don't get to be the most powerful man in the world without knowing *some* things.

It was like a dream. Maybe it *was* a dream. Lazlo's head was reeling with the news, and to Simon it looked as though he was about to keel over and wreck the tepee.

"Are you all right, Lazlo?"

"I don't know, said Lazlo. "I think I need an Alka-Seltzer."

While Simon prepared the Alka-Seltzer, Lazlo told him all about the phone call from Phineas Higgins. While it was a great honor to be chosen personally by Phineas Higgins to

save Tuesday Night Football, it was also an awesome responsibility. Tuesday Night Football had become part of the
American landscape, like apple pie and the flag and jingles.
What if Lazlo couldn't boost the ratings? What if Phineas
Higgins really did pull the plug? The happiness of millions
of people, not to mention Phineas Higgins, now rested
squarely on Lazlo's shoulders (which were broad, but not *that*
broad). What if he wasn't up to it? What if he couldn't make
all those people happy?

Simon hated it when Lazlo got introspective.

"Listen, Lazlo," he said with a trace of impatience, "I'm a
respected spiritual leader among my people. Would I shit
you? I'm telling you, this is the moment you've been waiting
for. The impossible dream that you're always yacking about.
Your moment of stardom. Fifteen years as the Jingle King,
busting your balls in piano bars and skull orchards…you
deserve a shot, Lazlo. Tomorrow night you're going to be up
there in the booth with Lance and Haywood and you're going
to play your jingles for the whole country. Isn't that what
you've always wanted?"

"Sure, as long as it makes everybody happy," said Lazlo.

"Of course it'll make everybody happy. Why wouldn't it
make everybody happy?" asked the Indian. "Lazlo, you may
be corny, but you're the best."

But Lazlo wasn't listening any more. He was lost in a
reverie.

"Geez," he said aloud to himself, trying to imagine it.
"Lazlo Horvath on Tuesday Night Football…"

# FOUR

**P**hineas Higgins was a man of his word. Lazlo found that out the second he stepped out of the tepee and encountered a paper boy hawking the morning edition.

"EXTRY! EXTRY! READ ALL ABOUT IT!" hollered the kid, looking just like a young Jackie Cooper in cocked hat and knickers. "Paper, mister?" he asked Lazlo, who was still trying to adjust to the blinding dawn light.

"Sure, kid. I'll take one," Lazlo said, flipping him a quarter. The boy hopped on his Schwinn and pedaled off, apparently headed for the next village some forty miles away.

Lazlo glanced at the newspaper and was amazed to see a banner headline proclaiming, LAZLO HORVATH NAMED TO TUESDAY NIGHT FOOTBALL, under which was a photograph of Lazlo and his accordion in action (not a very good likeness, really) and a story about Lazlo the Jingle King.

"Boy, news sure does travel fast around here," he said to

Simon, handing him the newspaper. The Indian had to concede that Phineas Higgins didn't waste time.

Neither did Lazlo. There was no time to waste if he was to save Tuesday Night Football from the Nielsen graveyard.

"You sure you won't come with me?" he asked Simon one more time as they loaded up Lazlo's Jeep with his indestructible Samsonite suitcase and his custom-made hardshell accordion case upon which was printed "Lazlo the Jingle King," just as it was on the sides of his Jeep. (I don't want you to get the idea that Lazlo had a big ego. In fact, just the opposite was true. It's just that being the Jingle King was his business, and if Lazlo knew anything at all he knew the importance of advertising. Besides, he didn't want people to confuse him with any other Lazlo, as if such a thing were even possible.)

"I'd like to go with you, Lazlo," Simon replied, "but there are some things you just have to do on your own. This is one of them. I'll drop you at the airport."

They got into the Jeep and sped off, Simon behind the wheel. He loved how the Jeep's four-wheel drive cut through the desert sand.

"I'm going to get me one of these things some day," he said.

"It gets twenty percent better mileage than the best-selling Japanese imports, you know," Lazlo answered reflexively; his mind was elsewhere. "The only thing that concerns me," he continued, "is that I don't really know very much about football. What if they want me to talk about the *game?*"

Lazlo, despite his awesome size, really didn't know much about football. He had never played the game—not even in high school—even though everyone was always trying to persuade, coax and shame him into going out for the team. But he would just patiently explain to one and all that he really didn't want to have to hurt anybody, and if he played football he didn't see how that could be avoided. He liked the game, though—what little he knew about it.

"You don't know very *much* about football?" asked Simon incredulously. "Lazlo, you don't know fuck-*all* about football. Samantha Laughing Dog knows more about football than you do!"

"That's what I mean. What if they want me to actually analyze the game or something?"

"Tuesday Night Football doesn't have anything to do with *football,* Lazlo. It's all about *television!* That's why they want you. You were made for the medium, and the medium was made for you! You're the Jingle King, Lazlo. One of a kind. Don't you ever forget that."

"I won't, kimosabe," said Lazlo, almost overcome with emotion. Simon was right. Lazlo *was* one of a kind. He *was* the Jingle King. That's why Phineas Higgins called him personally to save Tuesday Night Football, and why he couldn't let him down.

"Do you have any idea what 'kimosabe' means, Lazlo?"

"No," said Lazlo. "What's it mean?"

"It's Potawatamie for 'dumb shit.' Please don't call me 'kimosabe.'" said Simon.

"Okay," said Lazlo, who felt much better now that he knew what he had to do.

# FIVE

They rolled along the desert highway at breakneck speed while Lazlo hummed the Marlboro jingle. Whenever he was driving through the wide open spaces, he would hum the Marlboro jingle. He didn't know why. He would also hum it when he was particularly excited, such as when he was looking out over the mountains from the window of a Boeing 707, or roaring down the water slide at Six Flags. It was as though he saw himself in a movie, with all kinds of wonderful things happening all around him, and the Marlboro jingle was his personal theme song. Today was no exception. It could even be the greatest movie he'd ever been in.

He saw Ron and Nancy Reagan riding on horseback along the side of the road. Simon forced himself to slow down to avoid hitting them.

"How's it goin', Lazlo?" Ronnie called out with that big wave and "aw shucks" smile that kept him in political office for so long.

"Love to stop and chat, Ron," Lazlo called back as Simon jumped on the gas pedal, "but I'm late. I'm going to be on Tuesday Night Football!" His voice sounded like a siren going by (Simon wasn't a big Reagan fan).

"What'd he say, Mommie?" asked Reagan, cupping his ear as the Jeep whizzed by.

"He said they want him for Tuesday Night Football," Nancy replied.

"Why in heaven's name would they want *that*?"

"I don't know," said Nancy, "but he's such a nice man, isn't he? We should have had him as Secretary of something-or-other. Too late now, I suppose."

Ronnie agreed. It *was* too late. But that's another story....

Lazlo remembered the old days, when he had first come to the middle of Nowhere so many years ago, and how he would ride the bus to school every day with the bus driver trying unsuccessfully to stump him. He got out his accordion.

"Go ahead," said Lazlo. "Give me a really tough one."

"All right," said Simon, puffing pensively on his pipe. "Almond Joy."

"You mean, 'Sometimes you feel like a nut, sometimes you don't?'" Lazlo scoffed. "Come *on*, Simon. That's too easy. I've gotta keep my chops up!"

"Okay," said the Indian, accepting the challenge. "You'll never get this one. Cracker Jack."

Lazlo had to think about this for a while. He hadn't heard the Cracker Jack jingle in many years. Suddenly he looked worried.

"Gotcha," crowed Simon. "The Jingle King is stumped." He began to laugh like Woody Woodpecker. Lazlo kept thinking. You could almost hear the wheels grinding as he furrowed his eyebrows and tried to concentrate on the Cracker Jack jingle. Finally a big smile crossed his face and he cranked up the accordion and started to sing:

"Lip-smackin', whip-crackin', paddy-whackin',
inka-nappin', zilliga-lackin', scallaga-whackin',
Cracker-Jackin'... Cracker Jack!"

"You mean *that* Cracker Jack jingle, Simon, or were you thinking of another one?"

All right, you win," said Simon grudgingly. "You always do."

"Jingles are my life, Simon," he said, and he has never said anything truer before or since.

# SIX

**T**here was a great mob of people gathered at the TWA terminal of the Tucson airport when Lazlo and Simon arrived. Simon thought that they were there to give Lazlo a proper send-off, but it turned out that they were all just going somewhere and preferred to go there on TWA.

Lazlo bade Simon farewell and the Indian drove off in the Jeep, promising to be there waiting when Lazlo returned. In the midst of all the curbside confusion, with hundreds of anxious travelers trying desperately to be the first out of town, Lazlo never even noticed the person who bumped him and removed his billfold with all the skill and cunning of a Rumanian gypsy.

"Hi, Lazlo. Where you off to?" The voice sounded familiar. Lazlo turned around and was face-to-face with Karl Malden, who had seen him perform in many Holiday Inns across America.

"Chicago, Karl," said Lazlo. "I'm going to be on Tuesday Night Football!"

"Hey, that's great, Laz," Karl said with a familiarity reserved for old friends. "I always knew you'd make it big one of these days."

But all of a sudden there was serious doubt as to whether Lazlo was going to go to Chicago or anywhere else, for that matter.

"My wallet! My money! My credit cards! Everything— gone!" Lazlo was patting himself down frantically, working himself into a totally uncharacteristic panic attack. Wild-eyed, he was sweating profusely and hyperventilating, like a huge, claustrophobic child trapped in a darkened elevator. "What do I do *now*, Karl?"

Now he felt like a schmuck—not because he had had his pocket picked (all of us who have ever traveled to Italy have experienced that)—but because so many people were counting on him, whether they knew it or not. Without his credit cards he couldn't get to Chicago, and if he couldn't get to Chicago, Phineas Higgins would be very unhappy and Tuesday Night Football might very well be doomed and all its loyal fans left with nothing to watch on Tuesdays but sitcoms and cop shows, a fate Lazlo wouldn't wish on anybody. He remembered how Mirek Celinski and the Fabulous Polecats had broken up so many years ago, all on account of him, and his heart sank. He felt like a complete failure, a disgrace to his calling as the Jingle King. It was the only time I've ever heard of Lazlo coming unglued, but I think it was just the pressure of Tuesday Night Football.

God, they say, takes special care of widows, orphans and Lazlo Horvath. There's no other way to explain Lazlo's good fortune that Karl Malden happened to be at the TWA terminal that day.

"Calm down, Lazlo," said Karl in a voice ringing with authority, and Lazlo obeyed. "Every year, three out of ten vacations are spoiled by lost or stolen credit cards," Karl continued. "Fortunately, if you're careless or stupid enough to let your American Express card get lost or stolen, it doesn't have to ruin your whole trip. In most cases American Express can issue replacement cards on the spot."

"Really?" said Lazlo, instantly relieved. "That's terrific."

Karl reached into his pocket and pulled out a deck of American Express cards—green, gold and platinum.

"What color, Lazlo? asked Karl.

"Platinum," said Lazlo. "They always kind of liked me at American Express."

"*Everybody* likes you, Lazlo," Karl said as he thumbed through the deck until he found a platinum card with Lazlo's name on it. "Ah, here it is." He handed the card to Lazlo. "You don't have to worry about a thing. You can charge your tickets, insurance, hotel room, car rental—even get cash advances in more than twenty-two thousand locations world-wide. It's the only card you'll every really need, Lazlo."

"Thanks, Karl. I don't know what I would have done without you."

"You don't have to thank me, Lazlo. Membership has its privileges," said Karl.

"I've always known that," Lazlo replied almost reverentially. "I just wish they had a good, catchy jingle, don't you?"

"Why don't you write one for them?"

"Hey, maybe I will," said Lazlo. "Thanks, Karl. That's a real good idea."

"Enjoy your flight," Karl said, starting toward the gate. "And Lazlo, just one more thing..."

"You mean...don't leave home without it?" They both had a good laugh, and Lazlo was okay again. You can't stump the Jingle King, not even in a credit card crisis.

"What I was going to say," said Karl, "was, be careful. They'll kill you on television, Lazlo. The money's good, but they tear your heart out. They eat your soul. I should know."

"I'll try to remember that," said Lazlo cheerfully as they shook hands and went their separate ways.

Lazlo bought his ticket to Chicago, got some cash out of the American Express machine, and strode with a renewed spring in his step toward the security checkpoint, where hundreds of people were funneling into the only walk-through metal detector in the entire terminal. It was pandemonium, a riot in the making: Travelers of every age and description clawing, yelling, kicking and fighting to be first in line, acting very much like football fans.

None of this bothered Lazlo. He liked to see people who were enthusiastic about traveling. Besides, with that new American Express card in his pocket, he felt ten feet tall. He was Lazlo, solid citizen and Jingle King, and he was once again on his way to Chicago to be on Tuesday Night Football. He was truly blessed, and if he needed a reminder of that, it quickly came. Incredibly, as Lazlo approached the teeming, angry throng of people scratching and clawing each other at the checkpoint, the crowd simply calmed and parted, stepping aside to let him pass. He smiled at them and they smiled back, and he walked through the metal detector unimpeded, whereupon the mob resumed yelling and kicking and punching one another. Was it a sign of some sort? A divine gesture? An omen? I don't know, but I think the previous similar incident of that magnitude was the parting of the Red Sea, although I wasn't around for that and have only read about it.

(You're probably thinking that I'm either making this whole thing up or that I took a few too many head slaps during my playing days. Karl Malden at the Tucson airport with a fistful of credit cards? That's ridiculous. Well, maybe. Maybe not. I wasn't there, so I don't know. But I certainly wouldn't make it up. Lazlo was there, and to this day he swears it really was Karl Malden. As I told you, with Lazlo anything was possible. You'll just have to decide for yourself.)

Meanwhile, Lazlo got on the plane.

# SEVEN

Lazlo loved to fly almost as much as he loved jingles. From the moment he stepped on an airplane he was filled with an exhilaration that he could barely contain. From takeoff to landing, everything about flying was always exciting, no matter where he was going or how long it took to get there.

It also gave him time to reflect.

The American landscape was vast, beautiful and benign from 36,000 feet. The snow-capped mountains, starkly white, craggy and daunting, made him think of the intrepid pioneers who had settled this country against all odds, trying to realize their common dream of freedom and prosperity, refusing to conform or to be enslaved to someone else's vision. How he admired them! They had no jets in those days, no cars, no telephones, no television sets or jingles, no Tuesday Night Football. What did they have other than their courage, their families and their trust in one another, their feet, their pack mules and horses, their birchbark canoes and

Conestoga wagons? Were they ever really happy? If so, what made them happy? Lazlo thought of ants that spend their entire lives working to build their colonies, nothing more— tiny engineers hauling huge loads back and forth, back and forth, until they die. Their lives seem pointless, except that without their ceaseless work there would be no new generation of ants, and the whole species would vanish. Maybe that's how it was with the pioneers. Maybe their happiness was the whole point of their being here—to lay a foundation of civilization for their children and their children's children— and maybe that was what made them happy.

Lazlo had grown to love his adopted homeland for all of its beauty, all of its possibilities and all of its problems. Even the brutal cities, festering with crime and drugs and despair, looked like shimmering oases of golden citadels from the sky. He knew what was going on down there, and it broke his heart to see a great nation in decay. It was overwhelming. It was like watching a loved one slowly dying of cancer, and not a damn thing he could do about it except to try to make that loved one happy, even for sixty seconds. Why does death come disguised as progress, he wondered, and darkness pretend to be light? What would the pioneers say about what we have done to their legacy if they could speak to us now?

But never in Lazlo's lifetime had the world undergone such exciting changes. His country of birth, Hungary, still occupied a special place in his heart, for it was in his blood. And now Hungary had suddenly thrown off the mantle of oppression like an old rag, the people rising up and demanding their freedom. And they got it, the first free election in Hungary since Lazlo was two years old! And not just Hungary; the same thing was happening in Yugoslavia and East Germany and Czechoslovakia—all over Europe, millions of ants standing up, demanding to be happy, demanding to be free, demanding to be included in the hopes and dreams of civilized human beings. It brought tears to his eyes, tears of joy, because it meant that there was still time for the human race to awaken from its deep sleep and save itself. And it meant that his job, to make people happy, was now more important than ever before. He wouldn't disappoint them.

Lazlo got out of his seat and went up the aisle to go to the lavatory. Many of the passengers, none of whom he had ever seen before, greeted him enthusiastically, wishing him well on Tuesday Night Football. This made him very happy, of course, but still he had to wonder how they knew. He had only found out about it himself a couple of hours earlier. Then he saw it: In the magazine rack on the bulkhead was the current edition of *Sports Illustrated* with his picture on it! He was flanked by Haywood Grueller and Lance Allgood—two men he had never met in his life—and all three of them wearing their CBA blazers, microphones and headsets, smiling into the camera like the closest of friends (even Lazlo had to admit that that was weird). The headline blared: WHO'S THAT WITH LAZLO? Lazlo, forgetting all about the lavatory, took the magazine out of the rack and went back to his seat to discover whatever else he didn't know about himself. His admiration for Phineas Higgins was growing by the minute.

While he was engrossed in the feature article about his anticipated triumph as guest commentator on Tuesday Night Football, Lazlo was interrupted by a buxom flight attendant who looked and sounded very much like Mae West in her prime:

"Can I do anything for you, Mr. Horvath, or do you have everything you need?"

The obvious *double entendre* was completely lost on Lazlo, who had long ago given up on the idea of romance. "Call me Lazlo," he said. "Everyone does."

"All right…Lazlo," purred the flight attendant, showing some leg.

"You know what I'd really like?" asked Lazlo innocently.

"Just name it."

"How about a nice Lipton tea? Nothing quenches my thirst on a long flight quite like Lipton's."

"My, you really *are* the Jingle King!" said the flight attendant, who was genuinely impressed. "You sounded just like a commercial right then!"

"Oh, thank you very much," beamed Lazlo, who went back to reading about himself.

The stewardess nuzzled close and leaned over, displaying a little cleavage. She smelled just like lilacs, which is what Wanda used to smell like. "Listen, Lazlo," she whispered, "would you do me one special favor?"

Lazlo's eyes were riveted to her formidable and well-sculptured breasts. He gulped.

"I guess so," he stammered. "What would you like me to do?"

"When you see Lance," she said, "would you find out for me if it's really true?"

"If *what's* really true?" asked Lazlo, who didn't know if anything was really true any more.

"Oh, if it's really true you'll find out," she said coyly as she walked away, leaving Lazlo with just one more thing to wonder about.

# EIGHT

**T**he weirdness didn't stop when Lazlo's plane landed at O'Hare. If anything, it was only just beginning.

When Lazlo came out of the terminal, lugging his accordion and his trusty old Samsonite suitcase, he walked right into the worst traffic jam he had ever seen. It was like Rome, Paris, Athens and Cairo rolled into one. Horns were blaring, drivers shouting remarks back and forth about each other's respective parentage, buses belching noxious black smoke, cops handing out parking tickets as fast as they could write them. Utter insanity.

*Boy,* thought Lazlo, taking it all in, *it's great to be back in the city again!*

Off in the distance he saw two men with luggage running over the tops of the gridlocked cars toward the TWA terminal. They were clearly in a hurry. As the two men whizzed by it occurred to Lazlo that they looked just like O.J. Simpson and Arnold Palmer.

"I guess their Hertz contract must be up," Lazlo said to no one in particular.

A cabbie called to him: "Where to, Lazlo?"

Looking around, Lazlo thought he recognized the grinning cabbie, who looked remarkably like Magic Johnson. He went over to the taxi while Magic held the trunk open for his luggage.

"I don't know, Magic. They forgot to tell me what hotel I'm supposed to stay in."

"Well, don't sweat it, Lazlo," said Magic, whose natural state of happiness was impressive even to Lazlo. "Wherever it is, we'll get you there. Hop in."

Lazlo got in the back seat of the spacious Peugeot taxi cab and Magic roared off, deftly weaving his way through the stalled traffic.

"So what're you doin' in town, Lazlo?"

"I'm going to be on Tuesday Night Football!" Lazlo said with a grin almost as big as Magic's.

"Hey, all *right!*" said Magic. "That's CBA, isn't it? I know where all those folks are staying—right downtown at the Holiday Inn. Best hotel in Chicago, if you ask me."

"Holiday Inn's been very good to me," Lazlo agreed.

"You bet," said Magic. "Five-hundred rooms, cable TV, indoor swimming pool, tennis, racquetball, sauna, whirlpool, express check-out, kids under eighteen stay free with their parents—they even have a twenty percent businessman's discount Monday through Friday. Personally, I *always* stay at the Holiday Inn when I'm in Chicago. Be cool, Lazlo. I'll have you there in no time."

Soon they were on the John Kennedy Expressway, speeding toward the Loop at eighty-five miles per hour. They were going so fast that Lazlo didn't even see the huge billboard of himself modeling Vuarnet sunglasses; he was looking straight ahead.

"I'm a little nervous, Magic."

"Relax, man," said Magic. "This Peugeot's the best-handling import on the road. I *always* drive a Peugeot when I'm in Chicago."

"That's true," replied Lazlo. "It's the European car of the year. But it's not your driving I'm nervous about, Magic. I mean, what if I flub it? I've never been on television before, and everybody's counting on me. What if I make a fool of myself?"

"You ain't gonna make a fool of yourself, Lazlo. You're gonna be fine. Everybody *loves* you! You're the *Jingle King*, baby!"

As though Fate stepped in to punctuate the point, they passed a bus bearing an enormous picture of Lazlo with his soon-to-be colleagues, Lance and Haywood. It wasn't unlike the cover of *Sports Illustrated*. Lazlo couldn't remember when he'd posed for that photograph (he hadn't; his head had been superimposed on a picture of my body—without my permission, I might add).

"See?" said Magic, his teeth flashing like the keyboard of a Steinway. "What'd I tell you? Just remember, Lazlo, when you go up there in the booth, you're gonna be talkin' for all of us little guys everywhere. The fans. That's what it's all about—the fans."

"I know," said Lazlo, growing pensive. "Without the fans there wouldn't be any Tuesday Night Football. Or jingles, for that matter."

What he didn't say was that unless he did something to improve the ratings, there wouldn't be any Tuesday Night Football anyway. He didn't want his old pal Magic to have to worry about that.

Suddenly the Peugeot screeched to a stop in the middle of the expressway, and the G-force sent Lazlo flying ass-over-teakettle into the front seat, his legs wrapped around the meter and pressing straight up against the windshield. Behind them was the inevitable thirty-car pileup as all the other drivers tried (unsuccessfully) to stop and plowed into each other. It was a Cadillac massacre, but Lazlo, Magic and the Peugeot were miraculously unscathed.

"What happened?" asked Lazlo as soon as he could speak. Magic was remarkably calm, sitting behind the wheel and smiling.

"I always brake for animals. Don't you?" said Magic. Lazlo pulled himself up off the floor and looked out the window, expecting to see a cow or a buffalo, or at the very least a large, expensive dog. What he saw instead was a mother duck waddling across the freeway, followed by her brood of ducklings. As the crunch of metal on metal subsided, Lazlo could hear the faint "quack quack quack" of the feathered procession.

"Whew!" said Magic. "Thank God for these Goodyear steel-belted radials!"

# NINE

**W**hile Lazlo was nearly getting himself killed on the John Kennedy Expressway, little did he realize that others were plotting an even worse fate for him at the downtown Chicago Holiday Inn.

"What's a Lazlo Horvath?" Lance Allgood, waiting in the lobby for the elevator, looked idly up from his paperback copy of *The Joy of Sex* to see Lazlo's picture on the cover of the *Time* magazine that Haywood was reading. Lance, a former football hero and now the play-by-play announcer on Tuesday Night Football, was well-known to American audiences for his swarthy Dorian Gray good looks and his low-key, easygoing, midwestern guy-next-door on-air personality, but he was not noted for his keen grasp of current events. Ever since his divorce his single ambition in life seemed to be getting laid as often as possible with a variety of partners that would make Hugh Hefner blush. Lance *loved* women, and women loved him back. So much so that he never had to pursue them; women threw themselves at him like lemmings tumbling off a cliff—women of every size, shape, age, color and description found Lance utterly irresistible, and morning, noon and night he found himself in the unenviable position of having to try to satisfy their insatiable (and often bizarre) carnal appetites. It was a hopeless task but Lance did his best, for sex was as natural and necessary to him as breathing, an involuntary response.

"Our worst nightmare come true," said Haywood in response to Lance's question. Haywood Grueller, with his ratchet voice, Harvard vocabulary and rapier tongue, was the man everybody loved to hate, a caricature of himself who thrived on attention (even when it came in the form of letter bombs) and played it to the hilt. He was such an irritant to most people that they tuned in Tuesday Night Football just to yell insults at their television screens, and Haywood had become a rich man because of it. He didn't care what people thought of him so long as they thought of him, for he was very secure in the knowledge that he was the great Haywood Grueller and they weren't. Haywood was convinced that he was genuinely superior to everyone else and made no bones about it. (One thing I will say about Haywood, though: He spread his contempt evenhandedly; no one was exempt from the scathing disdain and stinging wit of Haywood.) Haywood Grueller was more than a household name; he was the object of universal loathing, and that suited him just fine. I always kind of respected him for that.

If there were two people in the world who weren't intimidated by Haywood, Yanya Zvornik was certainly one of them. Yanya didn't take any shit from anybody. The overachieving daughter of poor Yugoslavian immigrants, Yanya had seen enough in her thirty-some-odd years on this planet to walk through mine fields blindfolded at midnight. She had more balls than a brass monkey, and the kind of beauty that poets drool over. She was every inch her own woman (and what a woman!) and she never let anyone forget it. She was also the glue that held the show together—the associate producer, statistician, ringmaster, prevailing intelligence and last vestige of sanity for the whole production. Without Yanya there would have been no Tuesday Night Football. (Needless to say, if you've ever seen the credits at the end of Tuesday Night Football, Yanya's name goes by faster than the Wabash Cannonball. That's how it is in the macho world of television sports.)

"Apparently Lazlo Horvath is a fifth-rate lounge performer from Nowhere, Arizona," said Yanya, referring to her notes, "who plays the accordion badly..."

"As if to suggest anyone plays the accordion well?" offered Haywood as the three got into the elevator.

"Everybody loves him," reported Yanya. "*And,*" she continued, subtly letting Haywood know that she didn't like being interrupted during a briefing, "he claims to have an encyclopedic knowledge of every ad campaign ever launched. He bills himself as 'the Jingle King,' and Phineas Higgins, who apparently saw him play in Boise, Idaho, or someplace, has suddenly decreed that Lazlo's going to be the guest analyst on the show tomorrow night."

"Jesus, Mary and Joseph," intoned Haywood, who was Jewish.

"My sentiments exactly," said Yanya, "but I'm afraid we don't have anything to say about it. This comes straight from Phineas. He seems to think it'll hype the ratings in Yokelville or something."

"Hype the ratings!" said Haywood, disgusted at the mention of something so crass. "Has that man no shame? Tuesday Night Football is an American institution!"

"No, Haywood," Yanya corrected. "Princeton is an American institution. Sing Sing is an American institution.

Tuesday Night Football is a television show. And as long as Phineas Higgins pays the bills, if he wants a Lazlo Horvath on the air, then we'll *put* a Lazlo Horvath on the air."

"What's a jingle king from Arizona got to do with football, anyway?" asked Lance, still deeply engrossed in his book.

"C'mon, guys," said Yanya, "what's *any* of this got to do with football?"

"The woman raises a salient point, Lancelot," conceded Haywood. Then to Yanya: "What's Morton say about all this?"

"What do you *think* Morton says about all this? He's pissed off big time. The only thing Morton hates more than commercials is the accordion. 'Use an accordion, go to jail,' that's his motto."

"This may be the first time I've ever agreed with the man," said Haywood.

"But we still have to put this guy on the air, don't we?" asked Lance as they got off the elevator.

"So we'll put him on for ten seconds at halftime," said Yanya, who had the whole thing figured out. "Let him say hello to his mother or something and cut to the highlights. That way *he*'ll be happy, the *sponsor*'ll be happy, *Morton*'ll be happy...*we*'ll be happy. Everybody'll be happy, okay?"

Everybody agreed that that would be okay.

(It's a shame that Yanya knew so little about happiness. It's probably because of her childhood, but that's another story altogether.)

"Don't worry," said Yanya. "You guys do the game. I'll keep the Jingle King out of your hair. What the hell, it's only for two days."

"Uh...Yanya..." said Lance, gingerly testing hostile waters, "would you mind stopping by my room for a few minutes? I'd like to go over the spotting charts with you." (That was Lance's way of saying "I'd like you to come to my room, take off all your clothes and let me lick you from the bottom of your toes to the top of your head.")

Yanya smiled that drop-dead smile. "I'm sorry, Lance," she said sweetly, "but I have a hard and fast rule never to go to bed with any man who's prettier than I am. Nice try, though."

"Okay," said Lance, taking it very well, "see you tomorrow, then." He shrugged and went into his room to ponder a universal irony: Why was it that the only woman in the world he really wanted was the one woman he couldn't have?

# TEN

**P**oor Lazlo. I'm glad he didn't know that he was being sabotaged at the downtown Holiday Inn. He had enough problems as it was.

Magic turned onto Michigan Avenue and drove right smack into a shootout. There were cops everywhere—bullets flying in all directions, pedestrians running for their lives and diving under cars, a police helicopter circling overhead and television camera crews getting live coverage for the Five O'Clock News. Kentucky Fried Chicken was under siege.

The robbers rushed out of the building, machine guns blazing. Lazlo and Magic had to duck as stray bullets ricocheted off the Peugeot taxi cab, but they were in too much of a hurry to appreciate the danger they were in. The grin never left Magic's face.

"Traffic's a little heavier than usual today," he said. "Maybe I should find an alternate route."

"Good idea," said Lazlo, who watched the whole specta-

cle unreel like a Buster Keaton movie. As Magic tried to
maneuver the car through the tangle of traffic, one of the
robbers broke through the police barricades and, wielding a
.38 revolver in one hand and a bucket of Kentucky Fried
Chicken in the other, yanked the passenger door open in
hopes of commandeering the cab. He was suddenly face to
face with Lazlo, who smiled at him. The gunsel looked a lot
like Elisha Cook, Jr., in *The Maltese Falcon*. For some strange
reason Lazlo thought that the robber was offering him the
bucket of chicken.

"Hey, thanks, buddy," Lazlo said, taking the chicken and
closing the car door. Magic sped off before the gunsel could
shoot.

"Nice of that guy," said Lazlo. "I haven't eaten all day.
You like regular or extra crispy, Magic?"

"I prefer regular, myself," said Magic, careening around
stopped cars as pedestrians dropped like flies from errant
gunfire.

"Here you go," said Lazlo, passing him a drumstick.

"Finger-lickin' good," said Magic, savoring the chicken.

Lazlo agreed. "It must be the Colonel's special recipe
with his seven secret spices."

They munched as they drove out of the combat zone
toward the Holiday Inn and Lazlo's long-awaited rendezvous
with destiny.

# ELEVEN

**M**agic dropped Lazlo in front of the hotel with a final grinning admonition:

"All you gotta do is just be yourself and you're gonna do just fine, Lazlo. I guarantee it."

"Thanks for the lift, Magic," said Lazlo as he took his suitcase and accordion out of the trunk. "I'll be seeing you." Lazlo looked like a man on his way to the firing squad. His responsibility for the future of Tuesday Night Football was starting to weigh heavily on him. Not even the sight of King Kong swatting biplanes from the top of the Sears Tower in the distance could take his mind off the task at hand.

"Just remember what I said," Magic called as he got into the car. "Ain't nobody can beat you but *you*."

"Don't worry, I'll remember," said Lazlo as Magic drove off in the direction of the giant monkey.

Lazlo picked up his suitcase and accordion and trudged up the long driveway toward the hotel entrance, dodging the cabs that seemed to be trying to run him over. It was not an auspicious beginning to his one night of televised glory. A bell captain and about fourteen small bellhops were standing around the curb doing nothing, but no one made any move to help Lazlo with his bags.

"Could somebody give me a hand?" Lazlo asked, and the bellhops all broke into spontaneous applause. It was an old joke, but it made Lazlo laugh and feel welcome in Chicago.

"Just leave the stuff there, pal," said the haughty bell captain. "We'll take care of it. I trust you have a reservation?"

"Looks like he just *came* from one," said one of the shorter bellhops, cracking himself up. His sense of humor was obviously as retarded as his height.

"I'm going to be on Tuesday Night Football," Lazlo said, just in case they didn't recognize him.

"I'll notify the media," sneered the bell captain, who thought (incorrectly) that he was superior to Lazlo. He wasn't superior to *any*body, including the munchkins who worked for him.

"Oh, I think they already know," Lazlo said, not realizing that the man was being sarcastic. He put his suitcase and accordion down by the curb and walked into the hotel lobby.

And a grand lobby it was, too, with its shimmering crystal chandeliers, a marble-tiled floor covered by an enormous Persian carpet, replica Louis XIV furniture strategically placed around gigantic potted philodendrons, spectacularly gorgeous women everywhere, and a harpist in the corner playing the "Moonlight Sonata." Lazlo stopped to take it all in and was almost overcome by the grandeur. Somehow it reminded him of his father's mansion in Nowhere, Arizona, it was that elegant. All of a sudden he realized that he had finally *arrived*, and it sent shivers of excitement up his spine. This was the Big Time. Now, he thought, if he could only get the harpist to play some of his favorite jingles everything would be just perfect.

While Lazlo was gawking at all this opulence the bell-hops outside had gone back to their conversation, completely ignoring Lazlo's bags. They became so engrossed that they didn't notice the garbage men pull up and toss Lazlo's accordion case into the back of the truck and drive away until it was too late. When they realized it was missing they shrugged as if to say, "Well, what can you do?"

Lazlo saw Fawn Hall checking in and decided that he'd better do the same. But as he approached the desk he was intercepted by the hotel manager, who seemed to know who he was.

"No need to check in, Lazlo," said the manager, who had a pasty white complexion like a writer friend of mine and was wearing mourning clothes. The man bore an uncanny resemblance to Vincent Price, and his demeanor was grave. "He's waiting for you in room 2001. If you'll follow me..."

"Who is?" asked Lazlo.

"Mr. Finch."

"Oh," said Lazlo, his excitement growing as he followed the manager to a special elevator that required a key to operate. Lazlo had never seen Morton Finch, but he knew who he was, all right. He was the President of CBA Sports, the George Washington of Tuesday Night Football, probably one of the most important men in television. "He wants to see *me*? Wow! That's great!"

"Immediately," said the manager as the elevator door closed behind him. "He was rather insistent."

"You gotta get some sun, Vincent," said Lazlo, but the manager said nothing.

"I thought this hotel only had five hundred rooms?" said Lazlo, trying to make conversation.

"Room 2001 is a...*special* room," Vincent said, and Lazlo decided not to pursue the matter.

When they got out of the elevator they were in a long corridor that rated a perfect 10 even on the Lazlo scale of weirdness: It was dark and foreboding as a bat cave, contemporary Gothic, lighted only by flickering candelabras mounted on the wall. Vincent took one of the candelabras and led the way. Lazlo, quaking in his moccasins, meekly followed, clinging to Vincent's clammy arm. As they made their way along the creeky corridor, Lazlo was sure that he heard distant cries and moans. He was a huge mass of gooseflesh, too terrified to speak. Finally they arrived at the door to room 2001 and Vincent handed Lazlo the candelabra, as though passing the Olympic torch.

"Come in!" boomed a voice from inside even before Lazlo knocked. Lazlo gulped.

"Goodbye, Lazlo," said Vincent in his best undertaker's voice. "And good luck."

Lazlo turned to the door again, unsure of what to do. He wanted to be in Mozambique—Beirut—*anywhere* but where he was.

"Get *in* here, you idiot!" the voice from inside room 2001 bellowed. Lazlo turned pleadingly to Vincent, but Vincent was gone, having vanished without a sound. Resigned to whatever dreadful fate awaited him, Lazlo tried the handle and the door creaked open. He timidly stuck his head inside.

"Helloooo?" he called with the voice he used whenever he was pretty sure there were ghosts in the room. "Anybody home?"

# TWELVE

**L**azlo wasn't very worldly, I admit it, but during the course of his travels over the years he had been in quite a few hotel rooms. Never, though, had he ever seen one like this. Room 2001 was dimly lighted and as big as the Carlsbad Caverns. On every wall were banks of video monitors and enough electronic controls to launch a space shuttle. Some of the monitors displayed color bars, while others showed a test pattern. The main monitor, a fourteen-footer, completely covered one wall, and on it was the CBA logo, which was bigger than Lazlo. But there was no sign of Morton Finch or any other living soul, and the room was chillingly quiet.

Lazlo looked around in awe and wonder, then thought seriously about getting the hell out of there. *Saving Tuesday Night Football and making everybody happy is one thing,* he thought, *but this is getting too strange*. Then suddenly, just as he was about to leave, the monitors all switched to one picture. Lazlo nearly jumped out of his buckskins.

There, staring at him from every screen in the room, was the stern, unblinking, white-haired image of Morton Finch, looking somewhat like an angry sorcerer. Wherever Lazlo looked, there was Morton Finch looking back at him. He felt like he was trapped in a Versailles of fun house mirrors, being studied by a hundred all-seeing Big Brothers. He felt cornered like a rat.

"Sit down, Lazlo," commanded the various images of Morton Finch, and they meant it. Lazlo did as he was told.

"Do you know who I am?" the face in the monitors asked.

"You wouldn't be God by any chance, would you?" (Lazlo didn't really think that Morton Finch was God, but he had a feeling that if God ever did appear He would probably look something like Morton, and it would probably be on television.)

"Close enough. I'm Morton Finch, the executive producer of Tuesday Night Football. It's my responsibility to keep this catastrophe afloat."

"I'm awfully glad to meet you," said Lazlo, offering his hand before realizing that there was no one there to shake it. He felt a little foolish and retracted his hand.

"Let's get right to the point," said Morton, who didn't much like small talk. "None of this was my idea. As far as I'm concerned it's the most harebrained thing I've heard in thirty-two years of broadcasting. *But*, unfortunately I have to answer to our advertisers, and our advertisers are interested only in demographics. You follow me?"

"Yes, sir," said Lazlo, who was nervously trying to light his pipe. "I think so. You're saying that they want a lot of people to watch so they can sell their products during the game."

Morton didn't like having his explanations explained back to him. "Therefore," he continued impatiently, "you're going to be in the booth with Grueller and Allgood tomorrow night whether I have anything to say about it or not."

Lazlo had a little problem. In his nervousness he had spilled some tobacco embers out of his pipe onto the carpet, inadvertently starting a small fire. He got down on his knees and tried to pat the fire out without burning his hands, which he needed to play the accordion. He was sure that Morton couldn't see the fire because Morton was, after all, not really there.

"It's very exciting for me, Mr. Finch," said Lazlo, busily swatting the smoldering rug. "I even wrote a special jingle to do at halftime, if it's all right."

"No, it's not all right."

The fire spread to Lazlo's pantleg. He was hopping around like a one-legged man in an ass-kicking contest.

"The American people love jingles, sir. I don't want to let 'em down."

"Personally," said Morton with growing annoyance, "I happen to think the American people are out of their goddamned minds, but Phineas Higgins doesn't. So tomorrow night, this is what you're going to do: You're going to go into the broadcast booth with Lance and Haywood. You're going to put on a pair of headphones and you're going to sit there and watch the game like a graven image. You are going to speak only when spoken to, and you are going to say only what you are told to say by the director. Verbatim. You will make no spontaneous comments, you will offer no analysis, and you will sing no jingles at halftime or at any other time. You will not play the accordion, the glockenspiel, the gypsy violin or any other musical instrument. You will be a silent spectator, and by eleven-thirty you will be on your way back to your tepee in Arizona and I'll be able to hire Alex Karras like I wanted to in the first place. Are there any questions?"

"I see your true colors shining through, sir," said Lazlo, desperately looking for anything wet to put out his clothes.

"What the fuck is *that* supposed to mean?" Morton wasn't used to insubordination.

"Nothing, sir. It's the Kodak jingle. Don't worry. I'll do my best."

"Now put that fire out before you burn down the whole fucking building!" said Morton. Lazlo was rolling around on the floor in a futile effort to do just that. "Then get out of here. Breakfast meeting at eight o'clock tomorrow."

"What time was that, sir?" panted Lazlo, who was in great pain and not listening very carefully.

"Eight o'clock, you imbecile," said Morton. "Good night!" With that Morton's images simultaneously disappeared, the monitors all went to black and the fire alarm and sprinklers kicked in, creating a deafening noise and sending a Niagara of water cascading down upon Lazlo's half-scorched body.

When Lazlo finally made his way back to the lobby, soaked, singed and bedraggled, Vincent had Lazlo's new on-air wardrobe waiting for him.

"Mr. Finch insisted," said Vincent, handing over the clothes. "Dare I ask how your conference went?"

"Oh," said Lazlo, admiring his new red blazer with the CBA logo stitched over the breast pocket, "he's a terrific guy, don't you think? Very intense. We're gonna get along just great, I can tell."

Vincent looked at Lazlo like he had lost his mind, but Lazlo was too busy trying on the blazer to notice. It fit perfectly, as though it had been specially tailored for him. (It had been.) He stepped over to the mirror near the elevators to take a good look at himself, and what he saw made him very happy. *Welcome to Tuesday Night Football, Lazlo,* he said to himself as the other hotel guests walked past him at a safe distance.

# PART THREE

# Tuesday Night Football

# ONE

**T**he day dawned cool and crisp along the blustery shores of Lake Michigan, and the city of the big shoulders (as the poet once called it) rumbled awake like a crotchety but reliable old friend. For all the secretaries and teachers and bankers and lawyers and laborers and students, it was just another Tuesday in Chicago. For Lazlo it was the Tuesday of a lifetime.

There was a place set for him at the big round table in the center of the Holiday Inn conference room, but Lazlo wasn't there. He hadn't slept a wink the night before. Not because he was anxious about the Big Day, but because he had spent the entire night in an Oak Park landfill rummaging through two hundred tons of garbage, looking for his accordion. He had somehow managed to trace the garbage truck that far, but his desperate search for the priceless old *Soprani* had so far yielded nothing, and he was growing more and more concerned. How could he play his jingle on Tuesday Night Football without his accordion? (He never really believed for a second that Morton Finch was serious about his not playing the jingle; he just attributed Morton's reluctance to pre-game tension.) Of course he could always stop in a music store and buy another accordion with his American Express card, but the *Soprani* was far more than a musical instrument; it had come to be a part of him—an extension of his very being—not to mention his last remaining link to his old friend and mentor, Mirek Celinski. So Lazlo decided to continue the search, even though the sun was rising rapidly in the winter sky and the massive John Deere bulldozers were gearing up to undo all of his painstaking excavations. The breakfast conference, which was about to begin, completely slipped his mind.

"I don't suppose anybody's seen Lazlo," said Morton. "I *would* like to start this meeting sometime before I die." He was appearing courtesy of a small monitor placed neatly on the table between the silver setting where the breakfast plate otherwise would have been. Everybody else (except Lazlo, of course) was there in the flesh: Yanya, Lance, Haywood, and the director, Pete Gallo (who was no relation to Ernest and Julio, but probably wished that he was).

"He just called," said Yanya, who was typing her notes on a Toshiba laptop computer. "Said he'd be late. Something about losing his accordion."

"Good," said Morton's image, as stern as ever, "we'll start without him. What've you got, Haywood?"

Slowly and deliberately, Haywood snipped off the end of a big, black cigar with specially-made Abercrombie & Fitch clippers, lit up, savored the smoke, and blew it in the direction of the monitor. Everything was a ceremony for Haywood, a preamble to his next brilliant observation.

"Well, Morton," began the World's Foremost Authority, "considering the ineluctable fact that this contest augurs to be a monumental soporific bore..."

"In English, Haywood, if you don't mind," said Morton,

waving away the cigar smoke which had somehow gotten into the monitor and was making him sick.

"The game's gonna be a stinker, Morton," Haywood pronounced, "and I'm going to have to wing it, brilliantly as usual, to cover our collective asses. Nobody in his right mind gives a damn about the Bears and the Lions. The halftime show ought to be all right, though." (Of *course* the halftime show would be all right, Haywood was responsible for it.)

"Speaking of which," said Yanya, "what do you want us to do about this Lazlo character?"

"Let him say hello to Podunk and give him the hook," said Morton, who didn't even want to discuss the topic. "Thirty seconds, tops. And under no circumstances is he to play that accordion at halftime. I don't care if you have to make it snow in the goddamn booth. I *hate* the fucking accordion!"

"Consider it done. *You'll* have to deal with Phineas Higgins, though." Yanya was a nuts-and-bolts producer. She didn't like television politics.

Morton erupted: "Fuck Phineas Higgins! *I* run this fucking network, not Phineas Higgins! Who the hell does he think he is, foisting this idiot off on me?"

"The man who pays the bills?" ventured Yanya, even though she knew that Morton's question was purely rhetorical.

"I don't care *who* pays the bills!" Morton thundered. "The only person I answer to is A.C. Nielsen, by God. The bozo's gonna sit there with his fucking mouth shut and he's gonna *love* it!"

"Haywood and Lance'll keep it going, right, fellas?" Pete chimed in like a corporate cheerleader. A short, swarthy man with excessive chest hair, Pete was given to wearing expensive Italian shirts half-unbuttoned and a lot of gold chains because he thought (erroneously) that that somehow made him appealing to women and that someday he might actually be able to have sex with one. He was a man who was completely out of place in virtually any situation, but he was an expert boot licker, which is probably why Morton Finch allowed him to work for him.

"That's what they pay us the big bucks for," said Lance absently as he ate his scrambled eggs with his nose buried in *The Joy of Sex*. He was reading a particularly interesting chapter about Oriental foreplay and didn't want to be bothered.

Pete slipped his hand under the table and tried to cop a feel of Yanya's thigh, but she reflexively swatted his hand away before it even got close to the fabric. This was a tradition with them, a ritual that had been performed a thousand times before, and still Pete didn't get the message. Once again rebuffed, he quickly composed himself and cleared his throat:

"We've got another problem, Morton."

At that moment the door opened and there, standing in the doorway—*filling* the doorway—was a triumphant Lazlo Horvath, smiling from ear to ear. He had found his beloved accordion. All eyes were upon him and the room fell silent.

"Hi, everybody," said Lazlo. "Sorry I'm late. Had a heck of a time finding my ax."

He lumbered over to his place at the table, hefting his accordion case along with him. Aside from bumping into the buffet table and nearly overturning it, he arrived at his seat without incident. Even Lance interrupted his reading to observe this shy giant make his entrance.

Lazlo was a little dirty from the previous night's activities, and the accordion case emitted a strange and unpleasant odor, similar to that of decaying flesh. He put the case on the floor next to his chair and sat down, an eager participant in his first production meeting.

"You'd never believe where I finally had to go to find it,"

he said to his disbelieving audience. Nobody wanted to know, and nobody was about to ask.

Yanya broke the awkward silence. "I'm Yanya," she said, offering Lazlo her hand. He took her hand and shook it.

"I'm..." As Lazlo shook her hand his eyes met hers, and he was suddenly flummoxed. There was something in the way she looked at him that was soft and kind, yet strong and direct. Her Yugoslavian eyes were black as anthracite and clear as a beacon. They seemed to be smiling warmly at him, and his knees turned to silly putty. It was the first time in thirty-nine years that Wanda Pozniak was totally out of his mind—not forgotten, but as though she had never existed. Yanya was perfect. "I'm Lazlo," he said finally, not wanting to let go of Yanya's perfect hand.

"I know," said Yanya. "I've heard a lot about you."

"Save the greeting card shit for Christmas, guys," Morton interjected. "Now what's your problem, Pete?"

"The same problem we have every time," Pete whined. "ABC's got thirty cameras to cover a football game. What've *we* got? Eight! How the hell am I supposed to stay with the ball if either one of the quarterbacks decides to get creative tonight?"

"So let's do something about it," said Morton. "Yanya, get the owners down here."

Yanya got up and went to the telephone.

"What's *your* problem, Lazlo?" demanded Morton.

"Oh, hi, Mr. Finch," said Lazlo. "I don't have a problem."

"That's what *you* think," the boss corrected.

"Now I know what the big boys eat," Lazlo said, noticing the box of Wheaties on the table.

"Welcome to Tuesday Night Football," said Lance, offering his hand in a genuine gesture of acceptance.

"Thanks, Lance. It's hard to believe I'm really here."

Haywood was not eating his Wheaties, but rather Yanya's

Danish, which he washed down with a big gulp of water. (Haywood, who in his time had dined with presidents and kings, was addicted to junk food and anything sweet, and had developed the irritating habit of eating off everyone else's plate, as if his celebrity stature invested him with some special dispensation to be a pig.)

Haywood was tuning up for another oration. "Lazlo Horvath," he intoned, "virtuoso accordionist out of Nowhere, Arizona...king of the jingles, and the greatest master of iambic pentameter since the greatest of them all, the Bard of Avon himself, William P. Shakespeare. Welcome to the booth, kid."

He, too, offered his hand, and Lazlo shook it enthusiastically. "Thanks, Mr. Grueller. I'm honored to meet you."

"I know that," said Haywood. "And well you should be. But since we'll be...working together...sort of...you can call me Haywood."

Yanya returned to the table and something assaulted her nostrils. It was the accordion case.

"Something *die* in here?" she asked as tactfully as she could.

# TWO

If you're like most fans you probably think that football is a fairly simple game played by big, violent men according to a set of rules, and that television crews set up to cover the action and beam it to you live and unrehearsed. That's what Lazlo thought, too.

The respective team owners, having been summoned by Morton Finch, wasted no time getting to the breakfast meeting. They knew who buttered their bread, and it wasn't the twenty-two guys on the field. It was Morton Finch, who had more power than a Roman emperor because he (and he alone) decided which games to broadcast and he paid the freight. (The fact that he got the money from the advertisers didn't matter; he was the czar who decided how and where to spend it.) Tuesday Night Football, as Lazlo was about to learn, was a classic example of the tail wagging the dog.

But the owners knew that, and they didn't mind being wagged so long as the price was right. They were (understandably) very accommodating to Morton because they, like he, were businessmen. They couldn't have cared less about the *sport* of football.

"By the way, Morton," said one of the owners, "I was over in France last week and had lunch with Jacques Martand of Peugeot. He told me how delighted they were to be one of the new sponsors of Tuesday Night Football, but they're a little concerned about product identification in the American market. They're afraid nobody over here can pronounce the name of their car.

"I assured him that we weren't all idiots on this side of the water," he added with a conspiratorial snicker.

"Any microcephalic moron can pronounce Peugeot," said Haywood, even though no one asked his opinion.

"European car of the year," piped Lazlo. "A friend of mine says he drives a Peugeot every time he's in Chicago."

"*Quid erat demonstrandum,*" Haywood said. He liked to use a Latin phrase every now and then to ensure that nobody knew what he was talking about.

"I don't give a shit about Peugeot," said Morton for the record. "I drive a Lincoln Continental."

"So what can we do you out of, fellas?" asked the second owner, a tubby little man who looked like a hot air balloon. ("Do you out of" is a phrase often used by industrialists to signify that they know they're crooks, they know that *you* know they're crooks, and they don't care. That's how they got to be rich enough to own football franchises—by "doing somebody out of" something.)

Morton knew the code. "Pete's got his ass in a crack," he said. All eyes shifted to Pete.

"We can't cover the game properly with only eight cameras," Pete explained. "Any kind of long pass patterns and we're fucked."

*An interesting dilemma,* thought Lazlo, who was happy just to be a part of this television sports power breakfast summit.

Lance had the answer. "You know, when I was playing,

the way we used to take away the bomb was by setting up the zone defense. The quarterback either had to run the ball or throw short. *That* would solve the problem."

*Man*, thought Lazlo, *that Lance is a genius!*

"So, what if the quarterback throws over the zone?" asked Yanya, always the voice of reason. "Then you've got an automatic touchdown and we still won't be able to cover it."

*Wow*, thought Lazlo, *that Yanya sure knows her football. How could Lance come up with something so dumb?*

"So you guys just call your coaches and tell them to stay inside the zone tonight. That'll solve that problem." Morton was talking to the owners.

"I guess we can do that if it'll help," said the Bears owner. "All right with you, Barney?"

"Fine by me," agreed the Lions owner.

"Great thinking, Lance," said Pete, always looking to make brownie points.

Lazlo's head was going back and forth like a man watching a Ping-Pong match. "I always thought the long bomb was a pretty exciting part of the game, myself," he said.

"And who the fuck asked you?" demanded Morton.

"This is network television, Lazlo," Yanya explained patiently, as she would to a child. "We all have to compromise."

"Oh, we do?" said Lazlo. "I didn't know that."

Morton cut him off. "Good. It's settled. One other thing: We're going to need both teams' game plans so we can start blocking for the cameras."

"No sweat," said the Detroit owner as he got up to leave. "We'll have the coaches send them to the production office."

The Chicago owner started sniffing the air like a bloodhound. "Is there a dead animal in here or something?"

"It's just my ax," said a slightly embarrassed Lazlo.

"We still on for tennis at noon?" the Detroit owner asked the image in the monitor.

"I still owe you one, don't I?" said Morton, his way of

saying that he would allow the owner to think that he was one of the boys.

After the owners left, everybody (except Lazlo) looked straight at Yanya, and she knew exactly what they were thinking: Find a way to get rid of that accordion, or else.

# THREE

**Y**anya was caught in a terrible dilemma. On the one hand, she didn't want to hurt Lazlo because she wasn't that kind of a person. Then, once having met him, she had to admit that he seemed harmless enough, even if he did play the accordion. (Actually she kind of liked him, as she might a big, fuzzy old English sheepdog.) On the other hand she had a job to do, to produce a multimillion-dollar traveling circus called Tuesday Night Football, and she knew she was expendable.

(It shouldn't come as any shock to you, unless you've been living on Jupiter, to hear that television sports is a male-dominated business; for a woman to succeed, she has to be twice as smart, twice as capable, and half as outspoken as the man who pays her salary. That was Yanya.)

She wasn't about to cash in her career to spare Lazlo's feelings, no matter how much he might have had his heart set on being on the show. She had a mandate from the boss.

She tried to prepare him for the worst. "You seem like a

nice guy, Lazlo," she said, walking him to his room. "Let me give you some advice. Don't get your hopes up too high."

*Uh-oh*, thought Lazlo, *here it comes. She's going to let me down easy.* (He thought that she could read his mind and somehow knew that he was crazy about her. He was wrong.)

"I think you should know that Morton's not all that thrilled about your being on the show," she said by way of explanation. "He kind of feels that you were...forced on him...by the sponsor...if you know what I mean." She was trying to be delicate.

"Yeah," said Lazlo, "I sort of got the feeling that he wasn't very happy. Don't worry, though, he'll get over it." His smile was so innocent that Yanya wanted to scream.

"Lazlo, he's going to bust your balls!"

"No, he's not," said Lazlo serenely, as though he knew something that Yanya didn't. "I know he seems a little gruff, but I think he's probably a pretty nice guy deep down. Otherwise he wouldn't have been so successful."

"A *pretty nice guy?*" Yanya couldn't believe her ears. "Lazlo, he's Attila the Hun!"

"Really?" said Lazlo, who often took things very literally. "In that case we might even be related, because my great grandmother was a second cousin to the Attila family. They were very big in Hungary, you know."

Yanya laughed in spite of herself. "Boy, you really are a piece of work."

"Thanks," said Lazlo. "I like the Sprite in you, too."

Yanya decided to let that one pass; she wasn't used to being talked to in jingles.

"Here, let me help you with that," she said, reaching for his accordion case.

"No, it's okay," said Lazlo. "I've got it." He refused to give up his grip and so did Yanya.

"It's my *job*, Lazlo," she said through gritted teeth, tugging with all her might.

Finally Lazlo decided that if she wanted to carry his accordion so badly he might as well let her. "Okay," he said, "but I'm warning you, it's pretty heavy." He let go in mid-tug.

It was "pretty heavy" all right. The centrifugal force sent Yanya spinning 'round like an Olympic hammer thrower as Lazlo stood and watched in amazement. She looked like she was going to screw herself right into the floor. Finally the accordion flew out of her hands and Lazlo stared in disbelief as his cherished *Soprani* sailed through an open window and plunged seventeen stories to the bustling street below.

"Oops," said Yanya, sheepishly putting her hand to her mouth. "Oh, dear."

Lazlo couldn't bear to look, especially after he heard the horns honking, the brakes screeching and the crunch of metal.

"My ax..." he murmured.

"I'm *so* sorry, Lazlo," Yanya said softly. "It just slipped out of my hands. Honest."

(Well, she wasn't exactly telling the truth about the accordion slipping out of her hand, for she had planned to dispose of it all along. But she did feel bad about what she had done, especially after seeing the look on poor Lazlo's face, and for that I suppose we should be grateful.)

"Don't worry," she said. "We'll find you another one. First thing in the morning."

"Won't the game be over by then?" Lazlo asked.

"I'm afraid so," she said, hating (just for a moment) all the dirty work that goes along with being a television producer.

# FOUR

**M**r. Allgood, may I see you a moment?" She was an apparition—a goddess, a blond Aphrodite—calling to him from across the lobby of the Holiday Inn. Her nametag identified her as Ms. Peach, and she was in town for a plumbers' convention.

"Sure," said Lance, who hadn't been with a woman in several hours. He made his way through a group of Japanese tourists like an explorer blazing a trail.

"I have something to show you," she said as he arrived, and she meant it. "Can you come with me?"

"I guess so," said Lance, checking his watch. (I don't know why he checked his watch; time has a way of standing still when Lance is in heat.)

She led him to a vacant conference room just off the lobby. Once inside, she closed the door and locked it, then—without another word—began removing her clothes as fast as she could. She was in a frenzy. Lance watched in awe as Ms.

Peach revealed, part by part, her incredible body. Within seconds she was as naked as a jay bird, and Lance's eyes were as big as dinner plates.

"Don't just stand there," she panted. "I've got to have it."

"Have what?" asked Lance, temporarily forgetting why some people take their clothes off in the presence of total strangers.

"Oh, give it to me, Lance," she pleaded, tearing at his clothes and popping the buttons off his shirt. "I've got to find out if it's true. Don't make me wait any longer, I'm begging you!"

"Well, if you insist—" he started to say, but she jammed her tongue down his throat and rode him to the carpet, slobbering all over him.

"Oh, I *do* insist," she moaned. "I do, I do, I do, I do!"

(In the interest of good taste, I don't think I should describe in any detail what they did immediately after that. You'll just have to use your imagination.)

Their passionate animal sounds could be heard all the way to the lobby, where Haywood was surrounded by the group of Japanese tourists, who were busily snapping pictures of this international sports icon with their Kodak automatic 35mm cameras. Haywood was in his element, holding court as he preached the gospel according to Grueller to a captivated and adoring audience.

"As I was saying to Emperor Tojo the last time I was in your diminutive country," Haywood reminisced, "ostensibly for the heavyweight sumo championships—"

"Oooh, is it a touchdown yet?" Ms. Peach could distinctly be heard to say from behind the locked door of the conference room. By the sound of her voice Haywood concluded that she was very excited. "Oh, *please* say it is, say it is, oh, yes, oh yes! Oh my GAWD!" she cried.

"Ah, the poetry of love," crooned Haywood to the Japanese contingent, which bowed in jolly agreement. "In any event," he continued, deftly picking up the threads of an interrupted monologue, "I told your emperor that it took you enterprising people forty years, but you finally won the war. It wasn't so long ago that 'made in Japan' was considered a pejorative in this country, but now it's become a standard sorely to be striven for. You should all be very proud of yourselves."

The Japanese, who had been collectively hanging on Haywood's every lofty syllable, nodded and smiled blankly. Haywood finally realized that none of them spoke a word of English.

"Why am I standing here?" he said, disgusted with himself. "You people don't understand a single thing I'm saying."

The Japanese bowed in silent agreement; they didn't have a clue as to what he was talking about.

"Well, I really have to be going," said Haywood. "We invade Tokyo in five minutes. I wish I could say it's been delightful. Sayonara."

"Sayonara!" chirped the tourists in unison as they snapped more pictures of Haywood from every angle, but mostly of his back as he made his way to the desk.

He was almost run over by a bellhop who looked very much like Billy Barty. The bellhop was marching through the lobby carrying an AT&T portable telephone on a sterling silver tray.

"CALL FOR PHILIP MOR-RIS!" the bellhop called out to the assembled throngs.

Sitting by a huge philodendron was a man who bore a remarkable resemblance to Cliff Robertson. Hearing the page for Philip Morris, he put down his copy of *Business Week* and went over to the bellhop.

"Thank you," he said, reaching for the phone. "I'll take that."

But the bellhop wasn't about to let this impostor have the

phone. "You will not," he said indignantly. "I know Philip Morris. I've worked with Philip Morris. Philip Morris is a friend of mine. You're no Philip Morris." Whereupon he walked away in a huff, continuing to page his friend and colleague Philip Morris.

Haywood paid no attention. He was being accosted by a bearded man in a tweed suit and deerstalker cap who looked something like Foster Brooks and was obviously intoxicated.

"Shay," slurred the bearded man, "Are you by any chance Haywood Gru-gru-grueller?"

"Yes, I am, my good man." (As I said, Haywood loved recognition, and it didn't matter what form it took.)

"Well, I'm a, I'm a, I'm a—" The man seemed to be stuck in some kind of loop. His speech was strangely punctuated by hiccups, and his breath was potent enough to repel aliens. Haywood backed up a little bit.

"You're a what?"

"I'm a, I'm a, I'm a...I am...a big fan of yoursh," said the man, and he seemed to mean it.

"Wellll," said Haywood, smiling. "Thank you very much."

"You damn well *better* thank me," the man said, "'cuz I'm the only fuckin' fan you got!" And he staggered away, no doubt in search of someone else whose day could use some brightening.

Unfazed, Haywood turned to the hotel manager, who seemed somehow always to be on duty.

"My room key, if you would be so kind," Haywood instructed with just enough snobbishness to reestablish his lofty mystique, lest someone arrive at the false conclusion that he was a mere mortal.

"Yes, sir," said Vincent, handing him his key along with a sealed white envelope. "And this arrived for you while you were in conference."

The envelope was addressed to "Haywood Grueller—

Personal and Confidential," and the writing (more of a scrawl, really) appeared to be either that of a child or a mental defective. Haywood looked at the envelope curiously for a very long time. He held it up to the light in a futile effort to see its contents. Haywood knew that he had a lot of enemies in the world (even though he couldn't imagine why), and he had to be careful. Finally satisfied that the envelope didn't contain an explosive device, Haywood opened it.

TONIGHT YOU WILL BE PARALYZED FOR LIFE, the note announced in letters that had been cut out of magazines and newspapers and glued to the page just below a picture of happy, frolicsome, naked little cherubs. *A strange valentine indeed*, thought Haywood.

"Bad news, I trust," said Vincent, who was not one of Haywood's greatest admirers.

"Just the inevitable fan mail," said Haywood, who was certainly not about to give Vincent the satisfaction of knowing what was in the letter. "Would you be good enough to phone the FBI?" he added.

While Vincent placed the call Haywood was momentarily distracted by nature. More specifically, he was distracted by the sounds of the natural (and unnatural) animal acts being performed in the conference room by Lance and the lovely and demure Ms. Peach.

"Oh my god, give me the *ball*!" howled Ms. Peach loudly enough to be heard in Springfield, and the whole lobby fell silent. "Oh yes, oh yes, oh yes...*ball* me!"

At that precise moment, Lazlo (looking very overdressed in his new red CBA blazer) and Yanya stepped out of the elevator. They, too, heard Ms. Peach's call of the wild, and Lazlo stopped dead in his tracks.

"Holy shit, Lance!" screamed Ms. Peach. "Oh yes, oh yes, oh yes, oh yes, oh yes, oh there it is..." (It sounded like a distant piston. Lazlo thought of the Good 'n' Plenty jingle.) "Oh yes, oh yes, oh yes, TOUCHDOWN!"

Everyone in the lobby, with the exception of Lazlo, Yanya and Haywood, burst into applause. Even the Japanese tourists seemed to grasp the profound significance of the event that they had just overheard and cheered appreciatively.

Lance's voice soared from the conference room in a spirited baritone rendition of the University of Michigan fight song. "Hail to the Victors," and soon the other hotel guests were singing along with him.

"Lance's morning mating call," Yanya explained to Lazlo, who looked a little bewildered. "You get used to it."

"It *is* true!" squealed Ms. Peach, sounding very gratified to have this information.

"There's something about an Aqua Velva man," said Lazlo without a trace of envy, and even Yanya had to concede that he was right about that.

# FIVE

Later that morning, when Lazlo first saw the fleet of shiny black limousines lined up outside the hotel, he naturally thought that the President must be in Chicago, or at the very least the Pope was back in town. The presence of police escort motorcycles suggested that something of monumental importance was about to take place right under his nose, and apparently a lot of other people thought so too, because large crowds were gathering on the sidewalk to see what all the commotion was about. But the cars weren't there for any mere president or pope. No, this motorcade was far more important than that.

"What are all the limos for?" he asked Yanya as she was trying to assemble the broadcast team in the hotel lobby, which was full of CBA executives.

"Lunch," she said dismissively. Then, "Has anybody seen Haywood?" she called so that everyone in the lobby could hear her. She seemed frustrated, like a camp counselor trying to gather all the children together for an apple bob.

"I believe he's in his suite," said Vincent from behind the front desk, "conferring with the authorities. Shall I call him?"

"Authorities?" said Yanya. "What authorities?"

"I believe it's the FBI, Madam," said Vincent, who didn't seem particularly concerned.

"What is it *this* time? Another death threat?" said Yanya, annoyed.

"Apparently so, Madam."

"Everybody knows you can't kill Haywood without driving a stake through his heart and Haywood doesn't have one," said Yanya. "So screw the FBI. I've got a show to run here."

A short time later, a very satisfied Lance appeared, zipping his fly and energized for the work at hand. Then Haywood got off the elevator, accompanied by a burly man in a cheap suit who was wearing his FBI identification card over his breast pocket. It said his name was Ed Hoover.

"Good of you to make it," Yanya said to them, looking at her watch for sarcastic emphasis. "Who's this?" She was referring to the G-man.

"This is Edgar, the talking simian," said Haywood. "He's here to protect me."

"God help us all," said Yanya.

"Pleased to meet you, Mr. Simian," said Lazlo, offering his hand. "I'm Lazlo."

"Yes, I know," said Edgar, refusing to shake hands. "And don't think I haven't got my eye on you."

"Good," said Lazlo. "Be sure to watch at halftime. That's when I'm going to do my jingle. I think you'll really like it."

"All right, gentlemen," said Yanya, her patience wearing thin, "*if* you don't mind. Our transportation is waiting."

The network executives marched out of the hotel and

got into their assigned limousines. Yanya, Lance, Haywood, Edgar and Lazlo followed and made their way through the crowd of gawkers to a Lincoln super-stretch at the head of the motorcade. Lazlo was very impressed (he had never ridden in a limousine before).

Many in the crowd cheered for Lance, and some of the younger women swooned. Lance obliged them by waving back and smiling his famous All-American smile. Lazlo waved too.

"They love us in Chicago," Lance confided to Lazlo.

"Hey, Haywood!" yelled a voice from the crowd just as they were getting into the car. "Fuck you!"

Edgar, who perceived public profanity as a potential threat, froze in his tracks and drew his gun, pulling a bead on the whole crowd, looking for somebody to shoot.

"Try to be discreet, will you?" said Haywood to the fed. "These people have First Amendment rights, you know."

"Just doing my job, sir," Edgar replied without ever taking his eyes off the crowd. "Personally, I happen to agree with your detractors."

"And you call yourself an FBI man," said Haywood with obvious disdain. They got into the car and closed the door just in time to avoid being struck by an overripe tomato that splattered against the glass.

"The vicissitudes of celebrity, kid," said Haywood to Lazlo as they settled into the luxury of the Lincoln super-stretch. "Pay no attention to them."

"Hey, Lazlo, good to see ya," said the driver, who was looking through the rear view mirror. It was Jimmy the Greek.

"Thanks, Jimmy," said Lazlo. "Good to see you, too. I'm doing Tuesday Night Football."

"I know," said the Greek. "Just be careful what you say on the air."

"I don't think we have to worry about that," said Yanya, who had absolutely no intention of letting Lazlo say *anything* on the air other than "Hi, Mom."

The Honda police motorcycles roared into service and the motorcade crawled away from the hotel entrance, inching along Ohio Street through cheering (and jeering) throngs to its first destination—a Junior Chamber of Commerce luncheon four whole blocks away.

# SIX

They had only gone about half a block when Lazlo noticed something through the tomato-splattered window.

"Hey, Jimmy, hold it," he said with great urgency. "Stop right here for a second, will you?"

The Greek pounced on the brake with his Adidas shoe and the car lurched to a dead stop, nearly causing a twenty-car chain-reaction pileup as all the other limos stopped too. (Fortunately they were only going six mph at the time.) Yanya wasn't amused as the burly FBI agent plunged out of his jump seat into her lap.

Lazlo leapt from the limo and went over to the side of the road where his accordion case lay in the gutter.

"I found my ax," he called back to the other passengers by way of explanation.

He opened the custom-made Samsonite accordion case with some apprehension, fully expecting to see the wreckage of his cherished *Soprani*. What he saw, however, was an instrument that was perfectly intact, having survived a fall of seventeen stories. After pulling out some old dead cabbage leaves and chicken bones that were stuck in the bellows, Lazlo played a C scale to assess the damage. To his delight (and everyone else's horror) there was absolutely nothing wrong with the accordion except its aroma.

"It takes a licking and keeps on ticking," he announced with great pride as he carried it back to the car and quickly climbed in.

The smell was overwhelming. It was as though the accordion, during its night at the garbage dump, had absorbed all the foulest and most revolting odors known to the human nose the world over and combined them into one quintessential malodorous stench. It was like a musical toxic waste dump. Everyone in the car, including Jimmy the Greek (who was shielded by a glass partition), was crying profusely from the unrelenting stink, and Lazlo cried too, thinking that everyone was crying tears of joy because he had miraculously been reunited with his ax.

Finally the FBI man (who wasn't exactly a walking endorsement of Old Spice himself) couldn't stand it any longer.

"Possession of that instrument constitutes a federal offense," he said, snatching it from Lazlo and heaving it out the door before anyone had time to react.

"My ax!" said Lazlo, who was in shock over losing his accordion again.

"It's all right," said Yanya as she opened the sun roof and turned on the air conditioner, "we'll buy you another one. First thing in the morning."

Lazlo turned and looked forlornly out the back window as a vagrant spotted the accordion case and, thinking that he had made the score of a lifetime, opened it up—only to close it again and retreat to a safe distance as fast as he could, leaving the priceless *Soprani* in the middle of the street for some other victim to find.

They hadn't gone another block before all eyes in the limousine were on Lance, who was frantically pulling all his pockets inside-out. It reminded Lazlo of himself at the airport when he had his wallet and credit cards stolen. But this was even worse; Lance was out of condoms.

"Stop the car! Stop the car!" he shouted, pounding on the glass partition. "This is an emergency!" Jimmy the Greek, who was getting used to it by now, slammed on the brakes, and again the entire motorcade came within inches of a two-million-dollar multiple collision. They had been driving for twenty minutes and had traveled exactly eight hundred feet.

Lance got out of the limousine and went into the corner drug store. Haywood, who needed to stock up on Twinkies and toupee glue, decided to go with him. And where Haywood went, agent Hoover was sure to follow. This left Lazlo alone in the back of the limo with Yanya. It was a perfect opportunity to tell her how he really felt. That he was madly in love with her. That she had replaced Wanda Pozniak in his Hall of Fame of Perfect Women. He gathered all his courage.

"Listen... Yanya..." he began.

"What is it, Lazlo?" He imagined that it was the same tone of voice she probably used when she talked to her Dalmation when it woke her up in the morning with its leash in its mouth. Lazlo remembered what the doctor had told his parents so many years before when he wouldn't talk—that he wasn't a pet, that he needed attention. And for this moment he was a child again, and he needed attention more than ever. He needed Yanya's attention, for True Love was something Lazlo took very seriously (almost as seriously as jingles), even though his experience in such matters was limited.

"What *is* it, Lazlo?" she repeated when he didn't answer the first time. She sounded annoyed. "Can't you see I have work to do?"

He could see that, all right. Her nose was buried in her clipboard. She didn't even look up when she talked to him. He decided that maybe this wasn't the absolute best time to tell her that she was the woman of his dreams.

"Well," he said, "so far no one's told me exactly what I'm supposed to do when I'm up there in the booth." (He had to say *something*, didn't he?)

"You'll find out in due time," she said. "Just keep your pants on."

It was easy for Lazlo to keep his pants on. For Lance it was virtually impossible. While Lazlo was muffing his golden opportunity with Yanya, Lance was in the pharmacy face to face with a clerk who looked and talked just like The Great Gildersleeve.

"Yesssss?" said Gildersleeve as Lance fidgeted at the counter. "And what can I do for you?"

"I'd like a box of Trojans, please," said Lance in his TV voice. "And," he added with a whisper, "a pack of Camels." (His sexual escapades were a matter of public record, but he certainly didn't want anyone to know he smoked an occasional cigarette.)

Gildersleeve slipped him the Camels in a brown paper sack. "I'm sorry," he said, "but I'm afraid I'm all out of Trojans. I have all the other brands, though."

"No," said Lance, "I always use Trojans when I'm in Chicago."

"A condom is a condom," said Gildersleeve. "What's the difference?"

"And you call yourself a pharmacist," said Haywood through a mouthful of Twinkie.

"Haven't you ever heard of safe sex?" asked the G-man, who was leafing through a dogeared copy of *Penthouse* (which is probably the safest sex of all, come to think of it).

"I'm sorry," said Lance, and he *really* meant it. "There's no substitute for Trojans." (He wasn't talking about the college football team, either.)

"And remember," said Haywood, "you heard it from a connoisseur." He was holding up a tube of Crazy Glue.

"For the toupee, I presume," asked Gildersleeve, who could be almost as snide as anybody.

"Your perspicacity is utterly astounding," said Haywood, who could be even snider when the situation called for it.

When they left the drugstore, Lance was very concerned about his immediate sex life.

"Don't worry kid," said Haywood as they got in the limo. "I've got a Trojan in my wallet."

This got Yanya's attention. She was convinced that Haywood was too old for such tom-foolery. *That Haywood's quite a guy*, thought Lazlo, but he kept it to himself.

"A Trojan?" said Lance. "I've got the whole day ahead of me, Haywood. What am I going to do with one Trojan?"

"What you usually do, I would imagine," said Yanya.

Haywood took the rubber out of his wallet and handed it to Lance, who examined it like it was a foreign object.

"Haywood, this thing looks like it's twenty years old!"

"And then some," said Haywood, who seized upon the opportunity to explain the entire history of this particular prophylactic. "It was the 1962 Balkan Games. Bucharest, Rumania. A magnificently endowed Bulgarian shot-putter by the name of Svetlana Dimitrova proffered an assignation and I admit that this humble reporter was greatly tempted."

Lazlo was hanging on his every word.

"Commie scumbag," muttered Special Agent Hoover.

"Notwithstanding her politics," continued Haywood, "Svetlana was a stunning woman...who, unfortunately, turned out to be a stunning man posing as a woman, an indefensible charade which resulted in his disqualification from the games and a subsequent sojourn in Siberia.

"This unused Trojan is more than a condom, Lance. Consider it a monument to the unrequited romantic foibles of a naïve young sports correspondent, and wear it in good health."

"Wow," said Lazlo. "That's a fabulous story. You should tell it during the game, Haywood. I bet everybody would love to hear that."

Needless to say, Lazlo's suggestion was greeted with absolute silence.

# SEVEN

**B**y the time the motorcade arrived at City Hall for the Jaycees luncheon, the steps were lined three deep with Tuesday Night Football fans and rubbernecks, and the Richard J. Daley High School marching band was on the sidewalk playing a spirited, off-key rendition of "Send in the Clowns." (I personally think this was in very poor taste; Sondheim's songs were never meant to be played by marching bands.)

The broadcast team got out of the limo and walked regally up the steps on the red carpet which had been rolled out for them. Lance, Haywood and Yanya had done this a thousand times before, waving to fans in every NFL city except Phoenix, but of course Lazlo never had. And even in his wildest dreams he never thought it could be this good. He saw himself as a triumphant DeGaulle marching into Paris, General MacArthur striding ashore at Samar, Juan Valdez coming down from the mountains of Colombia. The people loved him—waved at him, cheered for him, blew kisses at him—and Lazlo waved and blew kisses right back. Every step of the way he floated on air. Lazlo, the Jingle King, the newest addition to Tuesday Night Football, was a hero in Chicago. The press descended upon him.

"Lazlo, just a few words," said a television reporter, thrusting a microphone in his face. "How's it feel to get a bigger reception in Chicago than the President got when he was here?"

"Well," said Lazlo, "the President has to make a lot of tough decisions. I guess he can't expect everybody to be happy all the time."

"Do you think you're going to have a problem working with Haywood tonight?" asked another reporter who was obviously trying to stir up trouble.

"No, why should I?" said Lazlo. "Have you had a problem working with him?"

"I never worked with him," said the reporter.

"Neither have I."

"Any truth to the rumor that Morton Finch hates your guts?" asked a woman correspondent from the *National Enquirer*.

"I don't think so," Lazlo replied. "I've only seen him on television. Seems like a pretty nice guy."

Yanya, Haywood and Lance all looked at each other in bewilderment; Lazlo certainly couldn't have been referring to the same Morton Finch that *they* knew.

"One last question, Lazlo," shouted a brash young sportscaster. "Who's gonna win tonight?"

"I don't know," said Lazlo, and he didn't. "But I always root for the home team, don't you? If they don't win it's a shame."

All the Chicago fans gathered behind Lazlo erupted into cheers at this last remark. Lazlo had won their hearts (but then it doesn't take much to win over the hearts of football fans with a few encouraging words about their team). Lazlo responded to the cheering with upraised arms and the victory sign, which just made them cheer louder.

He had stolen the show, all right, but not everyone was there just to see Lazlo. A stunning, statuesque black woman in a power suit approached Lance.

"Mr. Allgood? I'm Ms. Plum, director of public relations. I have a message for you. Could you come with me, please?"

Without a word, Lance followed. And why not? She looked exactly like Grace Jones. *Thank God for Haywood's Trojan*, he thought as he followed Ms. Plum through a gauntlet of rabid fans to a place of privacy.

# EIGHT

**L**ance's place at the table of honor was empty, but no one seemed to notice. Or care. Haywood was the main attraction, the Designated Speaker—the ringmaster—and it suited him just fine to have the floor all to himself. He was like a finely-tuned precision machine that could run on its own power indefinitely. He could go on and on and on about any subject under the sun, saying absolutely nothing at all, and making it sound so profound that his audience would sit in spellbound rapture, riveted to his every five-dollar syllable. (And, believe me, there were plenty of syllables whenever Haywood opened his mouth.)

Haywood's topic of the day, for some reason completely unknown to me, was boxing.

The banquet room of City Hall was an ocean of yuppies and their yuppie wives, each of whom had paid one hundred dollars to consume a silicone chicken, rub elbows with the Tuesday Night Football legends, and listen to Haywood pontificate. There were yuppies at the tables, yuppies on the dais, yuppies by the door. Yuppies everywhere. They were stockbrokers and investment bankers, BMW salesmen and insurance moguls, attornies, and arbitragers. They all had lots of money, perfect hair, car phones and beepers. They were all frustrated jocks (except for some of the wives), and they were there to get the inside scoop on Tuesday Night Football. The last thing they wanted to hear was a speech about boxing, but that's what they got. Sort of.

"This reporter's cardinal complaint with the American sports establishment as we know it," said Haywood in all of his stentorian, grandiloquent glory, "to which I could invoke an analogue for clarification…"

"Huh?" said one yuppie to his yuppie wife, who was equally confused and simply shrugged.

"There but for the grace of God goes God," sneered another yuppie, who was sitting on the dais with Lazlo and wearing a fake-fur Chicago Bears hat. This Bears booster was half in the bag and it wasn't even noon yet.

"He's great, isn't he?" said Lazlo, who was committing Haywood's every word to memory. "I think he makes a lot of sense." The yuppie looked at Lazlo like he was out of his mind (Lazlo, not the yuppie; yuppies never think they are out of their own minds). Haywood continued, gathering steam:

"…by comparing the state of professional sports in this country to the moral turpitude to which we are all bearing tragic witness of late vis-à-vis the economic cataclysm which we've brought upon ourselves with our myopic cupidity and for which we have none other than ourselves to blame.

"Case in point: While we are paying pugilists thirty millions of dollars a bout to indulge in an arguably barbaric pastime—"

"Blow it out your ass, Grueller!" yelled an irate yuppie from the back of the banquet room. "Boxing sure as hell made *you* a bundle!"

The FBI man, sensing possible trouble, drew his gun and took aim at the yuppie, just in case. The yuppie's wife was not amused.

"Sit down, Roger," she ordered. "Why do you always have to act like such a dork at these things?" Thus chastened, Roger did as he was told and Edgar put away his gun, but Lazlo noticed that neither of them was very happy about it. Haywood rolled on, barely missing a beat.

"—we at the same time allow thousands of poor unfortunates in each of our cities to starve. A sad commentary indeed. A perversion of values which portrays us as a nation willing to pay literally *anything* for our own entertainment while we cavalierly ignore the wrenching cries of our fellow citizens in distress. We think only of ourselves, the 'me generation.'

"And we call ourselves Americans," he added disgustedly.

"And I say you're full of shit, Grueller!" shouted the yuppie who was sitting next to Lazlo. He stood up, shaking his fist. "We don't have to take that from assholes like you! This is *America*!"

"He's just telling it like it is," said Lazlo to the yuppie.

Yanya was amazed by Haywood's remarks. In all the years she'd known him she never saw even a glimmer of humanitarian concern underneath that massive ego. *What's come over him?* she wondered. *Is he getting senile? Does he really have a soul after all?* For the first time in her memory she acknowledged that she actually almost liked him.

The yuppies didn't, though. Hell hath no fury like a yuppie reminded of his (or her) social responsibility. Even the CBA executives weren't thrilled with Haywood's topic of the day because they, too, were yuppies—television yuppies—and television yuppies have no stomach for social issues. We all know that television is strictly for entertainment.

Precisely how the brawl started I don't know, everything

happened so fast. There was a lot of booing and hissing at first, followed by mass table-pounding. Haywood waited for the demonstration to subside before proceeding with his speech, but the noise only grew louder. Edgar, the FBI man, quickly realized that he was hopelessly outnumbered and it would be pointless to shoot anybody. Besides, he was kind of enjoying the whole thing. The mayor took cover behind the podium as foreign objects were launched toward the dais—a few vases at first, followed by some dinner plates and poultry parts, culminating in a fusillade of wine glasses. Through it all Haywood stood his ground, stoically unflinching, as projectiles crashed all around him. (He had been a reporter long enough not to show fear in any situation. Besides, he was Haywood Grueller and they weren't.)

Lazlo hated violence. Violence made no sense to him. It was alien to his very nature, the exact opposite of everything he believed in, stood for and dedicated his life to, which was to make people happy. How could violence make anybody happy when the person on the receiving end always regretted it immediately and the person dishing it out usually regretted it sooner or later?

But when violence comes your way you have to respond, and Lazlo did. When the yuppie sitting next to him decided to escalate the proceedings by brandishing a Samsonite folding chair in the direction of Haywood's noggin, Lazlo stood and, with his meaty right hand, picked the man up by the scruff of the neck and held him suspended a foot above the floor. With his other hand he gently relieved the yuppie of the furniture he was holding.

"I don't think you really want to hurt anybody," said Lazlo politely while the yuppie pedaled furiously in midair. "Imagine how bad you'd feel tomorrow."

"Why don't you put him down, ya big palooka?" shouted a woman yuppie from the back of the room. But Lazlo had no intention of putting the man down until he no longer posed a threat to his new friend and colleague, Haywood.

"You gotta have the Jingle King along for a bodyguard these days, Grueller?" yelled another yuppie in the second row. Lazlo waved at the heckler, happy that he'd been recognized.

Haywood was not about to answer these barbarians, nor was he about to run for cover. Fortunately he didn't have to. From another room, like a supernatural sign, wafted Lance's clear, rich baritone voice singing the University of Michigan fight song, rising to a magnificent crescendo, and the mutinous yuppies fell silent. The voice had the purity of an angel's, the authority of a god's, and the yuppies forgot all about their assault on Haywood and began to sing along in rousing harmony, for U of M is the spiritual alma mater of yuppies throughout the midwest.

Thus, as quickly as it had begun, the brawl was over.

# NINE

**L**azlo was glad to be out of there. They were back in the limo, inching their way toward Soldier Field.

"Well, congratulations, everybody. I see you've managed to do it again." It was Morton's image in the limo's television monitor, and Lazlo could tell right away that Morton wasn't happy. "We could be the first network in history to be completely banned from a major American city. Can't you clowns go *anywhere* without getting in trouble?"

"Football's a violent sport, Morton," said a subdued Haywood. "It tends to attract violent people."

"Haywood's right, Mr. Finch," Lazlo volunteered. "That's the reason I've always stayed out of bars. Except when I was working, of course.

"By the way," he said to Haywood, "I thought your comparison of the excessive salaries of athletes to the nation's general economic and moral crisis was quite trenchant, to put it in your vernacular."

"Why, thank you very much," said Haywood. "I've obviously underestimated you."

"Put a sock on it, Lazlo," ordered Morton Finch. "You're just along for the ride, and I don't give a shit how fucking brilliant you think Haywood is. In fact, I don't care what you think about *anything*. Do your boot-licking on your own time."

"Okay, Mr. Finch," said Lazlo cheerfully.

Yanya, for some reason that she herself didn't quite understand, didn't like the way Morton was riding Lazlo, nor did she like the way Lazlo just seemed to take it. In her mind it was a gross mismatch and she didn't want to see anyone, not even Lazlo, reduced to rubble by this TV tyrant. (Which goes to show how little Yanya really knew about Lazlo at the time; no one could reduce Lazlo to anything.) She thought about speaking up, then thought better of it. *Better Lazlo than me*, she decided. She didn't want any part of Morton's wrath.

"And speaking of licking things, Lance," said Morton, "I would appreciate it if you would spend a little more time preparing for the show and a little less time trying to inseminate the entire female population of the western hemisphere."

"He doesn't really inseminate anybody, Mr. Finch," said Lazlo. "He practices safe sex."

"I always use a Trojan when I'm in Chicago," said Lance.

"I'll vouch for that," said Haywood, who thought the whole conversation was beneath his dignity.

"I don't care *what* you use!" said Morton, who was growing frustrated. "Boffing the director of public relations in the mayor's office is not exactly good for the corporate image of Tuesday Night Football!"

"She insisted, Morton," protested Lance. "What was I supposed to say—'no'?"

"You might try it sometime," urged Morton. "It would be a new life experience for you." Lance wisely let it drop. Morton turned his attention to Yanya.

"What other catastrophes await us today, Yanya?" (Morton more often than not thought in terms of catastrophe.) "And who's that asshole in the car next to you?" He was referring to Edgar, the G-man.

"The only other catastrophe I can think of is the game," Yanya said matter-of-factly. "And this asshole is with the Federal Bureau of Investigation."

"Special Agent Hoover, sir," said Edgar, introducing himself to the monitor in the limousine. "We've received another death threat against Mr. Grueller."

"Why wasn't *I* informed of this?" demanded Morton with great indignation.

"Because you're still a potential suspect, sir," said Edgar. "It's common knowledge that you hate his guts."

"*Everybody* hates his guts, you idiot!" said Morton. "Why do you think I keep him on the show?"

# TEN

It was a strange day in Chicago in more ways then one. As
though the television gods were smiling down on our happy
Tuesday Night Football production team, the wind suddenly
stopped blowing off the lake and the blustery winter weather
turned unseasonably warm. Indian summer had returned.

A sudden rise in temperature can cause problems, however, particularly when five people are bundled up in the
back of a limousine. It can get very...well...close. And
Special Agent Hoover, in his zeal and dedication to protect
Haywood, had apparently forgotten to bathe that morning.
(Personal hygiene was not high on his list of priorities.) The
combined odor of sweat and garlic emanating from his pores
was enough to pop the pennies off a dead man's eyes, as they
like to say in Ireland. (And he had the gall to complain about
the smell of Lazlo's accordion?!)

"Aren't you glad you use Dial?" Lazlo said to Yanya.

"Don't you wish everybody did?" she replied, casting a

not-so-subtle dagger-like glance in the direction of Edgar, who seemed quite unaffected by his own body odor.

"And you call yourself a public servant," said Haywood as he rolled down the window.

"Do you think we can stop at a music store along the way so I can pick up another ax?" Lazlo wanted to know. "Don't worry, you won't have to pay for it. I can use my American Express card."

"And I could use some more Trojans," said Lance, who was all in favor of stopping.

"There isn't time," said Yanya. "I'll have an accordion delivered to the booth, if it's all that important," she said to Lazlo, but she didn't mean it. She knew full well that she had no intention of doing any such thing.

"Oh, it *is* important," he said. "I can't do my jingle without it."

"Good," she replied. "And as for your Trojans, Lance, you're just going to have to abstain for a few hours or go bareback. We have an incredibly busy schedule today."

"But—but—" sputtered Lance. Never had a man been faced with two more horrifying alternatives. Lance go without sex for a few hours? Impossible. Not use a condom? Unthinkable.

"No buts about it." Yanya was unmoved. "They're shooting a Miller commercial at the stadium today and we have to pose for a few stills before we start blocking for the show. Every minute counts."

"You mean I get to see a real Miller commercial being made?" said Lazlo with childlike enthusiasm. "That's great. I bet they're a swell bunch of guys."

"Aren't you the lucky one." said Yanya.

"You can say *that* again!" Lazlo replied.

His excitement grew as they drove along the lakefront toward Burnham Park. Finally the stadium came into view, and Lazlo was almost overcome by its splendor. With its

classical Greco-Roman arches, Soldier Field rose up over the
lake like a defiant monument to what football is (or at least
*was*) supposed to be all about. No domed roof here, or air
conditioning, or plastic grass. No sir. When it rained you got
wet, and when it snowed you got cold. When the wind blew
(which was most of the time) anything was possible. Soldier
Field was the real McCoy, all right, with more than sixty years
of gridiron history swirling around behind those stately Doric
columns. Lazlo could almost feel the energy, as though the
old building had a life of its own, with its own story to tell.

"Soldier Field, kid—the last of the dinosaurs," said
Haywood nostalgically, revealing a wistful respect for tradition. It was an aspect of Haywood very few people ever were
close enough to him to see, and Lazlo felt honored to be
allowed to glimpse the softer side of the Man-Everybody-
Loved-to-Hate, however temporarily. He and Haywood were
going to become good friends; he just knew it.

When the motorcade arrived at the stadium entrance,
the CBA trucks were already in place, huge tractor-trailers
chock full of the most sophisticated broadcast electronics this
side of Japan. Cables ran out of the semis into the stadium
tunnels like huge, black umbilical cords.

The limousines kept going. At the other end of the
stadium, on the lawn of the park, was another cluster of
trucks, surrounded by a lot of people who were milling about.
Lazlo soon realized that this must be the film crew that Yanya
had mentioned, and his pulse quickened at the prospect of
actually watching them shoot a Miller beer commercial.
Jimmy the Greek stopped the car and they all got out as the
director told the camera operator where to set up for the
shot.

To Lazlo this wasn't just a commercial shoot; it was a
religious experience—almost a sacrament. He was a man
who had finally come home to his roots, for it had been
commercials that had molded and shaped him as a child and

had given the first real meaning to his life. He owed everything to commercials, including his understanding of what it meant to be happy. And he was happy just to be there.

Off to the side he thought he noticed two of his favorite television personalities, Billy Martin and Bubba Smith, studying their scripts. (Lazlo didn't realize that both Bubba and Billy, who had been great athletes in their time, weren't actually doing the commercial; they were represented by look-alikes, a sophisticated advertising ploy meant to cash in on the celebrity of famous people who didn't want to lower themselves to do commercials and thus to fool the average consumer, which usually worked.)

For this particular spot the Bubba look-alike, who was even bigger than Lazlo, was dressed in a gorilla suit (minus the gorilla head), and the Billy look-alike was in a safari jacket and pith helmet. They looked ridiculous, but Lazlo knew they would make him laugh.

Bubba was sitting in a director's chair outside the honey-wagon, muttering to himself, when Billy wandered up to him.

"Y'know, Bubba," said Billy, his face buried in the script, "we've been doing this same commercial for ten years and I *still* don't get it. I'm supposed to say 'tastes great' and you're supposed to say 'less filling,' right?"

"Right," said Bubba, who was sweltering and itching in the gorilla suit and really didn't want any part of analyzing his or anybody's else's dialogue. This wasn't art, this was television.

"And then what?" demanded Billy. "Is the audience supposed to think we really get into a fight or something?"

"How the fuck do *I* know?" Bubba replied impatiently. He tried to scratch his back under the gorilla suit, but he couldn't find a long-enough stick. "Jesus, it must be two-hundred fuckin' degrees in this thing."

Billy didn't care. He was engrossed in the motivation

behind the script. "But what are we supposed to be arguing about?" (Billy was tenacious, I'll say that for him.)

*Far out*, thought Lazlo. *These guys are really into their roles!*

"Who the fuck *cares* what we're arguing about?" said Bubba as all six feet nine inches of him stood up, dwarfing Billy. "Look, it says right here: You say 'tastes great' and I say 'less filling,' and it turns into a big fuckin' deal, okay? This isn't brain surgery, man! It's a fuckin' commercial, okay?"

No, it wasn't okay.

"Well," said Billy, who didn't seem to know when to stop beating a dead horse, "it seems to me that what they really want to say is that it's both less filling *and* it tastes great. But I certainly don't think it's anything to fight over, do you?"

"What the fuck are you askin' *me* for?" said Bubba, and he meant it. "I don't write this shit. Why don't you just try reading your lines right for a change."

(Ooops. Wrong thing to say, Bubba.)

"What's that supposed to mean?" Billy got very quiet, like a mongoose about to strike. (The fact that the top of his head came up just above Bubba's navel didn't seem to bother him. Or Bubba, for that matter.)

"Just what I said," Bubba growled. "You ain't got your lines right ever since I've been workin' with your sorry ass."

The camera crew and some of the extras moved in, forming a circle around them.

"They must be in the middle of a take," Lazlo whispered to Yanya, who wasn't so sure.

"Okay," said Billy, "how's this? 'Tastes fuckin' *great!*' How's *that*? Did I deliver *that* line okay, ya big, ugly *fuck*?" He was kicking dirt at Bubba's shins, even though Bubba looked nothing like an umpire in his gorilla suit.

Lazlo noticed that he didn't look very happy, either.

Rodney Dangerfield, among the crowd of onlookers, tried to intervene, "Fellas, fellas—" he admonished, but to no avail.

Bubba, who didn't like having dirt kicked on his gorilla outfit and being verbally abused, flew into an uncharacteristic rage. He threw a big roundhouse swing at Billy, who managed to duck. Billy countered by picking up some dirt and throwing it in Bubba's face, then tweaked the big man's ear and bopped him squarely on the nose for good measure. It was absolutely the wrong thing to do. Bubba went berserk, and Billy decided to run for his life.

"Oooh, Mickey. Stop them!" squealed Mickey Spillane's voluptuous bikini-clad girlfriend, sounding like a cross between Minnie Mouse and Betty Boop.

"I can't, doll," said Mickey, who knew a lot about violence. "It's part of the American male-bonding ritual."

Billy and Bubba took their dispute into the refreshment tent where Billy sought refuge behind the kegs of Miller beer. Bubba, hampered by his cumbersome gorilla suit, moved awkwardly, but there was no question in anybody's mind but that Billy was a goner the minute Bubba got his paws on him. The cast and crew loved it, yelling and cheering and egging them on. The assistant director started taking bets, and the odds changed every thirty seconds. Billy, the heavy underdog, hung in like a Tasmanian devil, picking up beer kegs one by one and hurling them at Bubba, who swatted them away with the ferocity that reminded Lazlo of King Kong, whom he had most recently seen on the Sears Tower.

The rest of the cast and crew also got into the donnybrook, breaking off into Billy and Bubba factions and bashing one another with every available object. (I have known film crews like this, believe me.) Soon beer kegs were flying in all directions, exploding on impact, and the tent was completely demolished.

"They make it look more real every time, don't they?" said Lazlo to Yanya.

"I hate to break it to you, Lazlo," she replied, "but it *is* real."

"It is?" he said. He looked over at Edgar the G-man.

"It's out of my jurisdiction," said Edgar, who wanted nothing to do with any of the combatants.

Lazlo decided to take the initiative. (*Somebody* had to.) He walked into the melee, seemingly oblivious to the danger he was in as phony kegs, tripods, folding chairs and camera equipment whizzed by his head.

"Lazlo, come back!" shouted Yanya. "You'll be killed!"

*Maybe she really does care,* thought Lazlo. He just smiled and waved back at her. He knew that no one would harm him because he meant them no harm.

"Come on, guys," said Lazlo, making the time-out sign, and everybody suddenly stopped fighting. (Why not? It worked for him at the Tucson airport.) "Commercials are supposed to make people happy," he said. "You don't seem very happy to me."

"We're not," said Billy, and he meant it.

"You better stay out of this, Lazlo," said Bubba, and he meant it, too.

"Okay," said Lazlo. "But it seems to me that the whole dispute can be settled without violence."

"I don't see how," said the director.

"Well," explained Lazlo, "half of you say it tastes great and the other half says it's less filling, and you're both right. It tastes great *and* it's less filling. So there's really nothing to fight about."

"He's right," said the assistant director.

"That's not what we were fighting about," growled Bubba.

"Oh, I'm sorry," said Lazlo. "I thought it was. My mistake. Don't pay any attention to me, then. Go on back to your fight." He turned and walked away, and for some reason nobody wanted to resume the brawl.

"What *were* we fighting about?" asked Billy.

"I don't remember," said Bubba.

"Well, fuck it, then," said Billy. "Let's get back to work."

"Okay by me," said Bubba.

"Places, everybody!" shouted the assistant director.

Arm-in-arm, Billy and Bubba returned to the honey-wagon while the crew began to clean up the carnage and attend their wounds.

Haywood, Lance and Yanya looked at each other in astonishment. *Who* is *this guy Lazlo?* they were all thinking at once.

"That was utterly amazing," said Yanya as Lazlo rejoined them.

"What was?" he said.

"What you just did. It was absolutely amazing."

"Oh, I didn't do anything," he said. "*They* did. As soon as they realized they weren't happy, they stopped fighting. Makes sense to me." And they had to agree with him whether they wanted to or not. In some strange, simple twist of Lazlo logic it all made perfect sense.

# ELEVEN

**L**azlo was anxious to get to the booth, even though it was still six hours until game time and he still didn't have the vaguest idea what he was supposed to do once he got on the air. Everybody was so busy and everything was happening so fast that no one had told him anything about his assignment. In fact, everyone seemed to be acting as though he wasn't even there. He felt a little like the Maytag repair man, but he knew that it was nothing personal. After all, Tuesday Night Football was a very complicated production requiring great preparation, and everybody had more important things to do than to think about him. He would just have to wing it for the time being, and be grateful just to be a part (however insignificant) of this legendary broadcast team. The electricity in the air sent shivers of excitement through his oversized body. He wished Simon could be there to share the moment with him, even if he wasn't quite sure what significance the moment held.

A security officer gave him a CBA staff pass and hung it

around his neck like a cowbell. "This'll get ya into any part of the facility," the security guy said. "Don't lose it or they'll throw you out on your ass."

"Oh, I won't," Lazlo assured the man, and suddenly he felt twelve feet tall. He could go anywhere in the stadium, and everywhere he went people would look at him and whisper, "Hey, there's Lazlo. He can go anywhere in the stadium." The sensation made him feel so good that he wished he could give one of those passes to everybody, so that everybody could go anywhere in the stadium and feel just as good as he did. But even though that wasn't possible, he was still going to play his jingle at halftime (assuming Yanya remembered to have a new accordion sent to him in the booth) and that would make everybody happy, which was probably just as good as giving everybody a stadium pass. Maybe better.

Lazlo followed Haywood into one of the production trucks parked outside the main entrance. Like a jolly, trusting earthling marching blindly into a flying saucer, he marveled at what he saw: Video tape decks, instant replay machines, editing and mixing consoles, a huge switching board and even more monitors than there were in room 2001 of the Holiday Inn. This was no ordinary tractor-trailer, Lazlo realized. This was the nerve center—the mobile electronic brain—of Tuesday Night Football!

Haywood sat down in front of a computerized console with an editor who looked to be about eighteen years old and together they began to assemble the halftime highlights tape from footage of all the games played the Sunday before. Lazlo stood off to the side of the editing bay and looked on as the old pro and the young pro scanned cassette after cassette, culling just the right highlights to create a dazzling three-minute montage of football action worthy of MTV. It was no longer Haywood the celebrity that Lazlo was watching, but

Haywood the consummate professional sports journalist. He was all business.

When the highlight reel was edited to Haywood's satisfaction, he picked up a microphone and began recording his voice-over. Lazlo was astounded by Haywood's uncanny ability to ad-lib, for there was no script in sight. He just made it up as he went along, describing each play like it was the greatest play he had ever seen, using that wonderful machine-gun delivery to make everything seem much more dramatic than it actually was on tape (or probably in actuality, for that matter). Haywood's voice was a unique instrument that could excite, anger, soothe or grate, depending on what effect he wanted to create at any given moment. He was truly a *maestro*, thought Lazlo, a verbal Paganini who played his own voice as well as Mirek Celinski ever played an accordion. And his timing was something to behold; without looking at a watch, without hesitating or missing a beat, Haywood recorded a perfect voice-over narration on the very first take.

"Boy, that's amazing," Lazlo said. "How do you do that without any notes or anything? How do you remember all that stuff?"

"It's a gift, kid." Haywood was gobbling a fistful of Cheez-Its. "Don't ask me how I got it, but whatever it is, I got it. Nobody can do what I do. And they call themselves professionals."

Lazlo understood. "Nobody can do what I do, either, Haywood. I guess that's why I'm the Jingle King and you're the Football King, right?"

"I suppose there might be some truth to that."

Haywood smiled. It was the first time Lazlo (or anyone else) had ever seen him smile. Even Haywood was surprised, and seemed a little embarrassed. He quickly resumed his normal demeanor before anybody else saw him smiling.

"C'mon, kid. We've got work to do." He gave Lazlo a friendly pat on the back.

"Y'know, Haywood," said Lazlo, "there's something I really don't understand."

Haywood took it for granted that there were *many* things Lazlo didn't understand. "What's that?"

"Well," said Lazlo, searching for just the right words, "I notice that an awful lot of people don't seem to like you very much."

"That's not exactly a state secret, kid," Haywood interrupted. He didn't seem to want another reminder of how many people hated his guts.

"But it doesn't make any sense to me," Lazlo protested. "From what I can tell, you're a terrific guy. You're a genius at what you do, you really *care* about people. If everybody could see the Haywood *I* see, nobody would hate you. They'd all like you."

This was precisely the last thing Haywood expected to hear, and he was momentarily stunned into silence. He'd been lazloed.[1]

"And I'd be out of a job," said Haywood.

"That doesn't make any sense," said Lazlo, who thought that everything should make sense. "You're the best. Nobody could replace you. You said so yourself."

"I didn't say that, kid. I said nobody can do what I do. *Anybody* could replace me. Even you."

Lazlo still didn't get it. "Oh, I wouldn't want to do that," he said.

"I was using an absurd example to illustrate my point,"

---

[1]**lazlo** (laz'-lo) **n.** an action reminiscent of or worthy of its namesake, Lazlo Horvath; e.g., "She did a lazlo and left the group dumbfounded."—**v.t. 1.** to make people happy whether they want to be or not; **2.** to perform such an action on another, often resulting in a dramatic change for the better without the other's awareness of what has happened; e.g., "After he lazloed her she never found fault with him again, though she couldn't explain why."—**lazloed, lazloing, lazlo-like.**

Haywood said. "Look, it's very simple. People don't turn on Tuesday Night Football to watch a football game, they turn it on because they're frustrated and they need someone or something to take their aggressions out on. That happens to be me. If people ever stopped hating me, they wouldn't have any reason to watch, because the football games, for the most part, are lousy."

"They are?" Lazlo didn't know that because he seldom watched Tuesday Night Football, and when he did he couldn't recognize a good game from a lousy one anyway.

"Of course they are," said Haywood. "In ten years we've done approximately a hundred and fifty games, out of which I'd say five were good. That's three-point-three percent. How many other shows could stay on the air for ten years with a success ratio like that?"

" 'Gilligan's Island'?" asked Lazlo.

"Another anomaly," said Haywood, who was talking rhetorically, not really asking Lazlo's opinion. "In any case, my job is to give people what they want. To be the object of their hatred and contempt."

"And you're very good at it," Lazlo said.

"Thank you. I'm flattered."

"Still, it's too bad they can't see all your good qualities," said Lazlo. "I bet they'd still watch."

"No. The minute they stop hating me, I'm a failure," said Haywood. "You think I enjoy being the butt of everyone's ridicule? Of having my face on dart boards and voodoo dolls? Receiving death threats every week? Listening to bad impressionists mock my unique locution? I have feelings just like everybody else," he added in a rare moment of candor. "But this is show business, kid. No show, no business. So as long as it's an opinionated, pompous ass they want, that's exactly what I'll give them."

"I see," said Lazlo. "I guess in a way you're a lot like me. You just want to make people happy, even if they hate you for it."

"I think you've said it very succinctly," said Haywood.

"Well," said Lazlo, "*I* don't hate you, Haywood. You're okay in my book."

"Try not to spread it around, will you, please," said Haywood, who was uncomfortable and really didn't want to talk about it anymore.

Fortunately he didn't have to. Due to some audio switching problems, Lance's voice could clearly be heard over the speakers in the booth, and everyone fell silent.

"You have the most incredible body I've ever seen," said Lance in a horny near-whisper. (Lazlo could only try to imagine whom he was seducing *this* time. It was kind of embarrassing, actually; Lazlo didn't like eavesdropping on somebody else's sexual encounter. He'd much rather participate, or at least watch.)

"We really fit together, don't we?" Lance continued. "I knew it the first time I ever got inside you—oh, inside you, inside you—it's like dying and going to heaven...."

"I can see why he's very successful with women," said Lazlo to Haywood.

"He's quite simply the best," said Haywood with unabashed admiration.

"...You're so soft, and you always smell so...sexy and feminine," Lance softly crooned. "And when we move together it's like poetry in perfect rhythm, isn't it? Oh, you are magnificent! And when I'm in you I never want the ride to end...."

"Do you think he knows her?" asked Lazlo.

"I wouldn't think so," said Haywood. "Lance tends to eschew sexual redundancy."

"...Oh, take me now," Lance implored, his voice building up to orgasmic intensity. "Take me wherever you want to go. Set me free and let me sing!" At which point his voice soared into yet another stirring rendition of the University of Michigan fight song that had become so familiar to Lazlo during the course of the day, and Lazlo was swept away on the vicarious wings of Lance's most recent ecstasy, his dulcet baritone trailing off into the ether to be replaced by another voice, an anonymous announcer's voice, urging:

"See your local Lincoln-Mercury dealer today and put the romance back into driving."

"Okay, CUT!" commanded yet another voice over the speakers, rudely jarring all the eavesdroppers in the production truck from their personal fantasies. "PRINT. Real nice, Lance. That's a wrap, everybody."

Lazlo looked over at Haywood, certain that he had been witness (sort of) to history being made. After all, he thought, who but Lance could make love to a woman and sell a car at the same time?

Ah, the miracle of television.

# TWELVE

If you've ever watched Tuesday Night Football (and who hasn't?), you probably know that "blocking" is a very important part of the game. Blocking is the strategy wherein gigantic men—helmeted, face-masked and securely padded from head to knee—grab, punch, kick, spit, poke, wrestle, grunt, curse, tear, gnaw, mangle, slap, smack, stomp, trip and throw one another to the ground so that a play might develop to advance the ball a few feet. Each such play lasts, on average, about six seconds, and during the course of the game this process is repeated over and over again until somebody eventually wins.

In many respects football is something like war, except that somebody wins football games and nobody wins wars. A lot of the terminology is the same, though: The "battle" is "fought in the trenches;" the "offense" tries to beat the "defense" often by "outflanking the enemy" or throwing the "bomb." The quarterback is known as the "field general" and

174

he, like most generals in real wars, is the highest paid, usually stays far away from the real fighting and seldom gets hurt, because he often wears a "flak jacket." And, like generals everywhere, when his team is triumphant he usually gets most of the glory. But enough of my opinion.

Lazlo was surprised to learn that there was another kind of blocking on Tuesday Night Football, and it took place long before the game ever began.

It was known as camera blocking, and it went like this: Several hours before the opening kickoff, Yanya and Pete would assemble the crack CBA technicians on the field, dividing them into two teams of eleven people each, and run different kinds of plays so that the crack camera operators could follow the movements of the players and the ball when the game was later played in earnest by real football players. (This kind of blocking is the same technique used by directors to choreograph everything from stage plays to television sitcoms; football apparently falls somewhere in between.)

The wall of Sony monitors in the production truck lit up and Lazlo watched this bizarre ritual unfold. The technical director sat behind his console of buttons, switches and faders, the master of all the equipment he surveyed, while Pete was out on the field, hooked up to a wireless microphone and headset which allowed him to issue orders to the camera operators who were strategically placed above and around the gridiron. (What a strange term *that* is! In all my years of playing football, nobody ever explained to me why they call it a "gridiron." I still don't know.) In any case, this little camera blocking exercise was Pete's weekly moment of glory, a time to recapture a high school fantasy never fulfilled, and for a few minutes every Tuesday afternoon he got to be the quarterback—the big cheese—the CBA Field General!

"Okay, let's see if you guys can keep up with the zone," said Pete into his microphone, " 'cause that's all we're gonna get tonight, assuming the coaches cooperate. We'll run five in a row."

He swaggered up to the line and stood over the center to take the snap of the ball. Yanya lined up at the tailback position, looking a lot better than any tailback Lazlo had ever seen in her Dr. Pepper T-shirt and spandex tights.

"Hut...hut...HUT!" barked Pete in his best Joe Montana impersonation. When the ball was snapped he dropped back into the pocket for a short pass play into the zone. Yanya ran out into the flat, then cut back toward the center of the field, criss-crossing the other receivers. Spotting her in the open seam, Pete fired off the hardest spiral he could throw— right at her chest. Unfazed by the velocity of the football (or its location), Yanya reached out and deftly hauled it in like it was a marshmallow.

"She's awfully good," said Lazlo, who was watching the whole thing in the truck and was more impressed with Yanya than ever. "Did she play in college?"

"No," said Haywood. "She idled away her time with academic pursuits."

"Good for her," said Lazlo, and he meant it.

When Yanya returned to the huddle, Pete (who was secretly miffed that Yanya had handled his hardest pass with the nonchalance of a Steve Largent) reached out and patted her on the ass, the way he thought macho athletes were supposed to congratulate teammates. Except that his motives were ulterior; he let his hand linger a little too long on her perfectly-formed posterior, and she didn't much care for it.

"Nice catch, baby," said Pete, who could single-handedly redefine the word smarm. "Maybe next time I should make it a little harder," he added with a coy snicker.

"Don't flatter yourself," said Yanya, who had been around more than one block and was familiar with lame *double entendres*.

"So what do I have to do to get in your pants—beg?"

asked the smooth-talking Pete, apparently unaware that his mike was open and he could be heard by all the camera operators, not to mention everybody in the truck and the Fuji blimp.

"But Pete," said Yanya, batting her eyes innocently, "what on earth would I do with *two* assholes?"

Pete wasn't amused, but he wasn't bright enough to spar with Yanya and he knew it. The crew stifled guffaws.

"That okay for you guys?" Pete was talking to the camera operators, trying to reassert his machismo.

"Looks good for camera one," said a voice in the headset.

"Looks great up high. No problem," said another voice.

"All right," said Field General Pete. "We'll run four more. See if you can pick 'em up."

Pete's team returned to the line of scrimmage and ran another mock play. Taking the snap, Pete faked a handoff to Yanya (copping a feel in the process) and tossed a little pass to the tight end on an eight-yard slant. Yanya, who didn't like having her breasts fondled by people she despised, said nothing as she walked back to the huddle plotting her revenge.

Since Pete was so fond of her breasts, she decided, why not give him a better glimpse? (Like most beautiful women, Yanya could be diabolical when the situation demanded it.)

Bending over in the huddle, Yanya made sure that the front of her T-shirt was open just enough to afford Pete the view of a lifetime. (Yanya's tits were so fabulous that I won't even describe them to you; you'll just have to use your imagination. An enterprising cameraman perched on the roof managed to get an extreme close-up of them, though, much to the delight of everyone in the production truck except Lazlo, who thought that it might be an invasion of Yanya's privacy.) Pete's reaction was exactly as Yanya had expected: He became so unnerved by the sight of Yanya's tits that he began to stammer and utterly forgot the sequence of plays. Yanya wondered how long it had been since he had seen a woman completely naked, let alone been with one. Then she decided that no self-respecting woman would allow herself to be seen completely naked by this man, let alone be touched by him. The mere thought made her skin crawl.

"Uh...let's see...uh..." Pete said, all the authority drained from his voice, his eyes bulging like a bullfrog's. Everybody stared at the Field General, awaiting instructions. He didn't have any. He'd lost it.

"Uh...what play should we run now, baby?" he asked Yanya.

(*Baby this*! she thought.)

"How about the flea-flicker?" she said sweetly.

"Sure. Why not?" said Pete, who was grateful for any idea at all. "We'll run the flea-flicker."

The "flea-flicker" is another football term that I have trouble understanding. I never figured out what it has to do with fleas, or flickers (whatever *they* are). But it is nevertheless a popular play among desperate teams, and it goes like this: The center snaps the ball to the quarterback, who hands off to the running back. When all the defensive players rush to tackle the running back, he pitches the ball back to the quarterback, who then throws it downfield—presumably to a wide-open receiver who has been ignored in all the confusion. When the play works it looks great to the television cameras and the fans. When it doesn't work everybody involved looks like a boob.

They broke the huddle and went up the line. Pete took the snap and handed the ball to Yanya, who waited until the defenders were almost upon her before she tossed it back to Pete. (Well, she didn't exactly *toss* it. She turned around and threw it at him with all her might.) It was a perfect spiral, traveling with the velocity of a heat-seeking missile, and Pete never had a chance. The end of the pigskin hit its intended target with pinpoint precision, scorching through Pete's outstretched hands and striking him squarely in the balls.

He dropped to his knees like a man who'd been shot as the pain exploded from his crotch and coursed through his entire body. His eyes bugged out of their sockets, as though he'd just seen the face of God. So profound was his agony that he sank to the ground in a writhing, whimpering heap, clutching his flaming scrotum.

"Jesus, I'm sorry, 'baby,'" said Yanya, barely controlling her glee. "Maybe next time I should make it a little harder."

"We missed that on camera six, Pete," said a deadpan voice in the headset. "You think you could run the play again?"

Pete tried to say something, but only hollow little squeaks would come out. Fortunately he couldn't hear the chorus of laughter that rocked the production truck.

As for Lazlo, if there was ever any doubt about his feelings for Yanya, they were completely erased now. If there was anything he admired (other than people who write jingles), it was a woman who could take care of herself in a man's world, and nobody did that better than Yanya.

# THIRTEEN

Lazlo was surprised to learn that not everything about Tuesday Night Football was first class. The pre-game meal for the production crew, served in the dank stadium cafeteria, could best be described as San Quentin *haute cuisine*.

"I don't know what it is, Haywood," said Lance as they all stood in the food line. "I just don't seem to have much energy lately." (This was ironic, considering there were jackrabbits in New Mexico that would be hard put to keep up with Lance when it came to sex.)

"Could be your diet, Lance," said Lazlo. "I've found that when we get to be a little older we have to watch what we eat."

Lance didn't want to watch what he was about to eat. It was too disgusting to look at. Lazlo noticed that the server looked just like Julia Child.

"Hi, Julia," he said. "May I have some of that, please?" He was pointing to a revolting concoction that vaguely

180

resembled some kind of stew. (Lazlo had grown up in Hamtramk, and could eat anything.)

"You can have whatever you want, Lazlo," said Julia in her familiar falsetto baritone as she heaped a big helping on his plate.

"Thanks, Julia," he said. "I want you to know I watch your show every chance I get. We should sit down and talk recipes sometime. I have a fabulous Dannon yogurt souffle that I'd like you to try."

"I'd love to, Lazlo," she replied. "Any time."

"I guess I'll have some of that, too," said Lance, against his better judgment.

"Six thousand dollars they spend transporting us to this godforsaken gridiron from a five-star hotel three and a half miles away," said Haywood, who was in fine form, "just to poison us an hour before air time. Would anyone care to explain *that* to this humble network servant?"

"It's a real puzzler, Haywood," said Lazlo.

"Julia Child," said Haywood, as though introducing her to a network television audience. "Boston's answer to Wolfgang Puck, empress of *nouvelle cuisine* and inspiration to gourmands the world over."

"Still full of it, eh, Haywood?" said Julia, who apparently knew Haywood pretty well.

"Does this excrescence have a name?" he asked.

"Of course it has a name, you silly billy," she said cheerfully. "It's called 'shepherd's delight,' and it's Mr. Finch's favorite pre-game dish. Goat's brains and minced mutton marinated in a mild vinaigrette with brown gravy and wild champignons. It's a real budget stretcher."

Lance put down his tray and vomited on the floor. The rest of the crew began banging their spoons and cups on their tables like extras in *10,000 Years in Sing Sing*.

"All right, you rats!" said the FBI agent, drawing his

revolver and looking for somebody to shoot. "That'll be enough! You'll eat this slop and like it!"

"And you call yourself a chef," Haywood said to Julia with unmitigated scorn as he pushed his tray away. "There's already been one threat made on my life today, and since I don't wish to be an accomplice to my own murder, I believe I'll abstain."

"But you must eat, dear boy." Julia seemed very concerned about Haywood's nutrition.

"Eventually, yes."

"Then how about some nice chocolate chip cookies?" she said. "I made them myself, especially for you."

Junk food—particularly chocolate chip cookies—was to Haywood what sex was to Lance: Something he had to have on a daily basis as often as possible. Of course he couldn't refuse.

"I offer my abject apologies, Madam," said Haywood in a clumsy effort to be gracious. "You are indeed a woman of taste, breeding and unparalleled magnanimity. Thank you *very* much." He snatched the box of cookies from her and began to devour them, refusing to share them with Lance or anybody else. (Lance didn't share his women, Haywood didn't share his cookies; it was the unspoken law of the booth.)

Lazlo sat down next to Yanya, who looked very glum. Her plate of shepherd's delight sat in front of her, untouched.

"Hi, Yanya," said Lazlo. "What's wrong? You don't look too good."

"*Men*, that's what's wrong. You're all a bunch of beasts." Yanya was stressed out; it was close to game time and she was sick and tired of Pete and everybody else trying to take liberties with her body, not to mention her mind.

"Well," said Lazlo, trying to cheer her up, "you know

what they say about men: You can't live *with* 'em and you can't shoot 'em."

Yanya didn't laugh. "Yeah, well, I can think of a few I'd like to shoot." Her venomous gaze drifted across the room and fixed on Pete, who was holding court with some of the cameramen whose jobs depended on pretending to like him. Lazlo was happy to see that Pete wasn't permanently incapacitated, even though he did seemed to be holding his nuts a lot.

"Just because some guys might be jerks doesn't mean that *all* men are no good," Lazlo said to Yanya. "A fabulous woman like you should have a man in her life."

"I'll take a pass, thank you," she said. She was in no mood to concede that a man was good for anything other than scalping.

"Okay," said Lazlo, who certainly didn't want to argue with the woman he secretly adored. "If you say so. But you're gonna miss out on a lot of good fucking."

Yanya shrieked, threw down her napkin and ran from the room. She was over the edge.

"Jeez, I hope I didn't say anything to make her mad," said Lazlo as he watched her disappear into the cavernous stadium.

# FOURTEEN

I have met some cruel people in my travels, but Lazlo is certainly not one of them. In fact, I've never known Lazlo ever to hurt anyone intentionally in his whole bizarre life, and this instance was certainly no exception. Nevertheless, Yanya was hurt and Lazlo felt in some way responsible. And, being Lazlo, he couldn't do the sensible thing and just let it drop. No, he had to follow her out of the cafeteria and try to make amends for whatever he might have said to make her so unhappy.

He found her crying in a stall in the women's restroom and knocked gingerly on the door.

"Yanya...?"

"Go *away!*" she shouted between sobs, and she meant it. "Can't a woman get any privacy *anywhere* around here?"

"I'm sorry, Yanya," he said gently to the door. "I didn't mean anything by what I said. Honest."

"Go *away!*" she screamed, and Lazlo was lucky that the

ladies' room was otherwise empty, or this whole situation could easily have been misconstrued.

"All I was trying to say," explained Lazlo, "is that you're too young and smart and beautiful to give up on men. You've got your whole life ahead of you, and believe it or not, there really are some good men out there."

Lazlo heard what sounded like a Canada goose honking, but it was just Yanya blowing her nose.

"Don't tell me you're coming on to me, too," she said, as though such a thing were impossible to fathom. It was.

"Coming *on* to you...?" Lazlo was shocked.

"All men ever want to do is *fuck* me!" she shrieked. "Ever since I was fifteen years old! I can't *take* it any more!"

Lazlo was beginning to realize that Yanya's state of mind was not just the result of a bad day with Pete. It was the cumulative result of a lifetime of bad days with a thousand Petes, and she was on the verge of cracking up.

"Why does every knucklescraper in the world only want to jump on my bones?" Yanya demanded.

"*I* don't," said Lazlo, and he meant it. There was a long silence from inside the stall as Yanya let this information sink in. She could hardly believe her ears.

"You don't?"

"No, I don't," Lazlo repeated, but not in a way to make her feel rejected. She felt rejected anyway.

"Why not? Is there something the matter with me?"

"Of *course* not!" Lazlo reassured her. "I think you're a wonderful woman. Even better than Wanda Pozniak. But..."

"But what," she sniffed.

"But...can't we just be friends?"

There was no answer from inside the stall, and Lazlo was afraid that he had inadvertently said something to make Yanya unhappy again, and he searched his mind for an appropriate line from a jingle that would cheer her up. But before he could think of anything the door opened and Yanya stood facing him with a semi-glazed expression. She was magnificent in her vulnerability. Then, without warning, she threw her arms around him and burst into tears.

"*Now* what did I say?" asked Lazlo in his bewilderment.

"No man ever wanted to be my friend before," sobbed Yanya, and at that moment Lazlo came to understand something very strange and wonderful about women: That their need to be respected almost always outweighs their need to be desired. Just like men.

Yanya was just about to confide her whole sad life story to her new friend and confidant when Julia Child rushed into the ladies' room with a sense of urgency usually reserved for such places.

"Oh, hi, Julia," Lazlo said, but Julia blew right past them into a vacant stall without saying a word. Lazlo and Yanya decided that they'd better vacate the restroom before Julia got the wrong idea.

After they were gone and Julia was sure she was alone, she went to the mirror and began tugging and clawing at her face like a crazy person in a frenzy of self-mutilation. But it wasn't *her* face she was tearing off; it was a rubber mask which happened to be a perfect likeness of Julia Child. And when the mask came off the results were very scary indeed: This woman—this shameless imposter—was one of the ugliest human beings God ever created. (There was a rumor that she once tried out for the role of one of the witches in Macbeth and was refused the part because she was too ugly, but I wasn't there, so I don't really know if it's true.)

Having discarded the Julia Child prosthesis in the trash can, the impostor changed into her street clothes and hurried from the lavatory. The threat to Haywood, which nobody (including Haywood and his FBI bodyguard) had taken very seriously, was genuine, all right, and this woman (whoever she was) was the culprit. And she didn't want to be anywhere near that stadium when Haywood bit the dust.

# FIFTEEN

**F**ifteen minutes to air, everybody." Yanya was in her producer mode, a woman in control of the situation.

Lazlo put on his headset and sat down on his stool facing a small monitor. (There was a little monitor for each of them; it reminded Lazlo of the waiting room of the TWA terminal in the Dallas-Fort Worth airport.) From the booth he could see everything that was happening on the field below, and he was tickled pink. It didn't occur to him that his headset and microphone were switched off in the truck and that he couldn't hear anything except what was said in the booth, nor could he be heard.

Haywood, who was still gobbling the chocolate chip cookies, assumed his place on a stool that was slightly higher than the others. He strapped on his headset and Lazlo noticed that Haywood's microphone was attached to a special wire harness that made it project straight toward his mouth. It looked like a giant dildo with a windscreen, but Lazlo didn't think he ought to comment on it.

"You hear me all right, Haywood?" asked Pete, who was in the production truck and had apparently recovered the lower register of his voice after his brush with disaster.

"His master's voice," grumbled Haywood, who somehow seemed a little odd, even by Lazlo's standards.

" 'His master's voice.' RCA. That's a good one, Haywood," said Lazlo. Haywood ignored him.

"Loud and clear, Pete," he said, eating another cookie.

"Talk to me, baby," said Pete, trying to be hip. "We need some levels."

"Pietro Gallo," intoned Haywood, biographer of the world. "The oldest son of Calabrian immigrants. Grew up on the wrong side of the tracks in the poorest section of Martha's Vineyard behind a squalid little shoemaker's establishment. Dropped out of school in the fifth grade to support his eleven brothers. Later earned notoriety as director of Tuesday Night Football. What a success story, ladies and gentlemen. Where else but in this great nation could a man with no money, no education and no talent—a quintessential mediocrity—rise to near greatness? I ask you."

"Thank you very much, Haywood," said Pete, who didn't know if he was being complimented or not. "Freeze logo on two," he said to the engineer beside him.

"Pete?" said Haywood.

"Yes, Haywood?"

"This humble announcer is ready."

"I'm delighted to hear that, Haywood," said Pete. "We're on the air in two minutes."

"Where's our spotter?" asked Haywood, who suddenly realized that they were one body short in the booth.

"He quit," said Yanya. "Went to work for Metropolitan Life."

"Get Met—it pays," said Lazlo reflexively.

"How are we supposed to identify the players without a spotter?" asked Lance in something of a panic.

"You might try watching the game," said Yanya.

"And you call yourself an associate producer," said Haywood, who was inexplicably starting to slur his words. Lazlo noticed that Haywood was also wobbling slightly on his stool.

"No, Haywood," said Yanya. "That's what Morton calls me. I call myself a producer, and if you don't believe it just stick around." There was fire in her eyes, and Haywood wisely decided not to pursue the issue.

"I'll be the spotter," volunteered Lazlo. "What's a spotter do?"

"We'll go without a spotter," said Pete. "After the intro we'll come in on the three of you. Lance, Haywood, give me about thirty seconds each, introduce the Jingle King, let him say hello or something, then we'll break for commercial."

"Morton's not going to like that," said Lance, looking at Lazlo. Lazlo, oblivious to what was being said about him, gazed smilingly at the huge crowd below and waved to some of his fans in section thirty-one. He was happy as a clam.

"So we cut him off after ten seconds," said Pete.

The engineer rolled the music tape, Pete cued Lance, and Tuesday Night Football was on the air. In the monitor in front of him, Lazlo saw a great overhead shot of Soldier Field, Lakeshore Drive and half of the Loop. *Wow*, he thought, *being here is just like watching it on television!*

"From the Fuji blimp 'Corumbia,' high above Soldier Field and the Windy City of Chicago, welcome to another edition of *Tuesday Night Football!*" said Lance, reading from a card. Lazlo couldn't believe how smooth and natural-sounding the man was.

"Tonight a battle of arch rivals as the injury-riddled Chicago Bears take on the Detroit Lions in what promises to be a classic Central Division matchup," Lance continued, trying to make it sound exciting. "Tonight's game is brought to you by...MAXWELL HOUSE COFFEE..."

"Good to the very last drop," said Lazlo.

"...And by...CHEVRON, and your local Chevron dealers," said Lance.

"We fuel your freedom," said Lazlo.

"What the fuck was that?" said Pete to the engineer.

"Beats me," said the engineer. "Sounds like that Lazlo guy." (It was; his voice was leaking through Lance's microphone.)

"...And by...EVERYTHING, INCORPORATED," said Lance.

This sent a tingle up Lazlo's spine; if it weren't for Everything, Inc., he wouldn't be on Tuesday Night Football. "You're nothing without Everything," he said, louder this time. "Everything brings everything to you."

Pete switched on Lazlo's headset and microphone as they rolled the stock Tuesday Night Football opening, a spectacular computer-generated animation featuring Lance, Haywood and (you guessed it) even Lazlo in a glitzy production that had nothing whatsoever to do with football but promised lots of excitement.

"Can you hear me, Lazlo?" said Pete through gritted teeth.

"Oh, sure, Pete," said Lazlo. "I can hear you fine."

"Then shut the fuck up, you putz!" said Pete, who liked to sprinkle his profanity with Yiddish even though he was Italian. "We're on the fuckin' air!"

"Okay, sorry," said Lazlo. "I didn't see the red light."

Whereupon Pete killed Lazlo's mike and ate a whole tube of Rolaids.

"Good evening again, ladies and gentlemen," said Lance, looking directly into the camera. "And welcome to Chicago. This is Lance Allgood along with my good friend and colleague, Haywood Grueller. We could be in for a pretty good game tonight if the warm weather holds, but here on the shores of Lake Michigan you just never know from one minute to the next what you're going to get."

At that moment a great blast of snow blew into the booth, nearly knocking him over and dislodging Haywood's toupee.

"And you see what I mean," said Lance. "What are your thoughts on tonight's game, Haywood?"

The cameraman focused on Haywood, who was standing on a box to appear taller next to Lance. His rug was still askew and his eyes had a kind of glaze to them. He seemed very disoriented for some reason.

"You're absolutely right," he said after a very long silence. "The weather could be a factor. As for the teams. The Chicago Bears and the Detroit Lions. Two also-rans, playing for pride. Not a pretty sight. Both teams out of contention, but seething with hatred for one another. But let's tell it like it is. On Tuesday Night Football anything can happen and usually does with these cunning little monkeys." Haywood was teetering precariously on his box, and Lazlo was prepared to catch him if he fell.

"Quick, go to Lance," said Pete, who didn't like what he saw. "What's got into Haywood? He's starting to make sense."

"Beats the hell out of me," said the engineer with a shrug.

"Lance, introduce the Jingle King," said Pete into Lance's headphones. "We need forty-five seconds."

"We also have a very special guest with us in the booth tonight," said Lance without missing a beat. "Lazlo Horvath—the man you know as the Jingle King—from Nowhere, Arizona. Come on in here, Lazlo."

He pulled Lazlo into the shot, but Lazlo's attention was on Haywood.

"You okay, Haywood?" he said, not realizing that he was being watched by millions of people. "You look a little peaked."

"I'm fine, kid," said Haywood, but he was visibly wobbling. Lazlo turned to the television camera.

"Hi, everybody," he said with a big smile and a shy little wave. "I'm Lazlo."

"Any predictions on the game, Lazlo?" asked Lance to kill time.

"Naw," said Lazlo, "I don't really know very much about football, except that it's kind of exciting."

"This is gonna be a long fuckin' night," said an obviously pained Pete to the engineer. "Give me an Advil."

The engineer handed over the bottle of Advil and Pete took them all.

"But let me tell you folks out there something," said Lazlo. "These fellas—these guys—Lance and Haywood, and Yanya over there, and Pete down in the truck...and Mr. Finch...they are the most wonderful people in the world, and CBA is the most wonderful network in the world, and I'm thrilled to death to be here tonight along with them. I just wish you could all be me right now, it's such a great experience." He looked at Lance. "You mind if I say 'Hi' to my friend Simon?"

"I think you just did," said Lance, trying to be cool. Then he abruptly changed the subject. "Tell us, Lazlo, why do they call you the Jingle King?"

"Because I do jingles, Lance. That's all I do. I just...what can I say? I just love 'em. Some people do Elvis, some people work in cheese factories—me, I do jingles. You name the product, I'll give you the jingle. Jingles are my life."

Lazlo turned to the camera. "In fact, I wanted to do my own jingle at halftime that I wrote especially for this occasion, but I lost my accordion, so I might not be able to do it after all."

He turned back to Lance, who was dying inside. "Say, you remember this one, Lance? 'YOU'LL WONDER WHERE THE YELLOW WENT," he sang, "WHEN YOU BRUSH YOUR TEETH WITH PEPSODENT."

"One of my all-time favorites," said Lance, but he didn't really mean it.

"Mine, too," said Lazlo. "You wouldn't believe how many requests I get for that one."

"Well," said Lance, "I'm sure we'll hear much more about it later on. Meanwhile, the Lions have won the toss and have elected to receive. We'll be right back with the opening kickoff right after these messages."

The red light went out on the camera and the booth was filled with the heavy reggae beat of a jingle for the Jamaica Tourist Board. Lazlo bopped along with the music (he particularly liked reggae music), and he didn't hear Morton Finch, who was talking into Yanya's headset:

"Would somebody mind telling me what in the name of God is going on over there?"

"No problem, Morton," Yanya lied. "Everything's fine."

"Not from where *I* sit, it isn't!" (He was sitting on his yacht down in Key West.) "Now I'm not going to say this again. Park that goofball somewhere and put a gag on him. If you geniuses can't do the show, I'll get somebody else who can. Is that clear?"

"Yes, sir," said Yanya "It couldn't be much clearer."

Lazlo noticed Morton's angry god-like image on the main monitor, and although he couldn't hear what Morton was saying, he got the impression that he was disturbed about something. *Probably the bad ratings*, he thought.

"Hi, Mr. Finch," said Lazlo, waving to the monitor. Morton growled like a man about to go berserk, then his image left the monitor so quickly that it looked to Lazlo like his head had exploded.

"Boy," said Lazlo, "he sure does get around, doesn't he?"

Yanya merely shook her head. She didn't have the faintest idea how she was going to make it through the night.

# SIXTEEN

**T**rue to Haywood's earlier prediction the game went south in a hurry. The Detroit receiver, Bebe Rebozo, ran back the opening kickoff 103 yards for a touchdown while the Chicago players stood around like fenceposts.

"And they call themselves 'the Monsters of the Midway,'" sniffed the semi-comatose Haywood, who was propped against the back wall of the booth to keep his knees from buckling as he ate one chocolate chip cookie after another. Lazlo was concerned about him; he had never seen a man wear a toupee over his ear before.

Eight seconds later the Lions scored another touchdown when the Chicago receiver, Nelson Eddy, fumbled the Detroit kickoff on his own two-yard line and Jamaal McDonald picked up the football and waltzed into the end zone.

By the middle of the first quarter the Lions had scored six touchdowns for a 42-0 lead.

"If they keep scoring at this rate," said Lazlo, "we're going to run out of commercials. What'll we do *then?*"

After that nothing happened. I mean *nothing*. For a quarter and a half, neither team could move the ball more than seven yards on any three consecutive plays, and there was a distinct possibility that an all-time record for punts would be established that night. After the initial scoring orgy, the game had become, as Haywood had prophesied, "a monumental, soporific bore."

"It looks like this is going to be some night," said Lance, looking over to Haywood for some trenchant comment. But Haywood was in no condition to make any comment, trenchant or otherwise. He fell face down on the floor of the booth like he'd been poleaxed.

"Oh my god!" cried Yanya. "Somebody get a doctor in here! Haywood's croaked!" (To this day I've never understood why people always call for a doctor after they think somebody's croaked. It seems a little late to me. But that's another story.)

"Go to commercial and pre-roll the replay," said Pete to the engineer. He was panicked and it was the only thing he could think of doing to stall for time. I mean, it wasn't every day that Haywood dropped dead in the booth, but the show still had to go on.

During the commercial break Lazlo leaned over and passed his hand in front of Haywood's eyes, which were rolled back in his head like pinballs. "Hi, Haywood. Anybody home?"

"I love you like money, pal," said Lance to his fallen comrade, "but if we have to go mouth-to-mouth, you ain't gonna make it."

"Holy shit, he's dead!" said Yanya, who was crying and had temporarily forgotten all about the show. Lazlo saw how much affection Yanya really had for Haywood, despite everything she had ever said about him, and it made him glad to see it.

"He's not dead," said Lazlo calmly. "He's just a little stoned, that's all."

"*Stoned*!?" said Lance and Yanya at the same time. They were incredulous.

"*Stoned*!?" yelled Pete through the headphones. "What the fuck's going on up there?" He was confused.

"Haywood's down, Pete," said Lance. "He's completely in the bag."

"It's nothing to worry about," said Lazlo. "I've seen my friend Simon like this millions of times, only with him it's a religious experience. Don't worry, Haywood'll be fine after a good night's sleep."

"A good night's sleep!? We've got a goddamn live show to do!" Pete was shouting so loudly that Lazlo's earphone almost leapt off his head, but it wasn't Lazlo's fault that Haywood was down for the count, and everybody knew it.

"How'd he get stoned?" said Yanya. "That isn't like him at all." She smelled a rat.

Lazlo took the last remaining chocolate chip cookie from the box and examined it closely. There was certainly nothing unusual about its appearance. Then he took a little bite, and he knew immediately how it had happened.

"*Sensimilla*," he announced with the authority of a wine connoisseur. "Northern California. Humboldt County, I'd say. My friend Simon says this is the best grass there is. Even better than Maui Wowie." (Lazlo was speaking clinically, of course; he'd had no personal recreational experience with the substance, in case you're concerned.)

"How come he didn't give *me* any?" Lance asked rhetorically.

"Twenty seconds," announced Pete. He didn't want to hear about the relative merits of Hawaiian and Humboldt grass. He needed somebody to call the game, in case anybody was still watching.

"Listen, Lazlo," said Lance, "You gotta help me out." There was desperation in his voice.

"Sure," said Lazlo. "What do you want me to do?"

"I've had a very rough day and I'm exhausted," Lance replied. "I can't carry this turkey by myself."

"Oh, I think he'll be all right where he is," Lazlo said. He was referring to Haywood, who was lying in a puddle of his own drool on the concrete floor of the booth.

"I mean the *game*," said Lance. "I just can't do it by myself."

"Of course you can!" said Lazlo. "You're the best play-by-play man there is. Everybody knows that."

"But nobody cares about that," said Lance, and he was absolutely right. "They want a show, and Haywood's the showman. Without him there is no Tuesday Night Football. Face it, Lazlo, without Haywood I'm almost as boring as this game. I'll put *myself* to sleep if I don't get some help in here."

"What do you want me to do?" said Lazlo. "I can't do any jingles without my ax."

"I don't care what you do," said Yanya. "Just keep talking."

(Yanya didn't yet realize what a dangerous thing she was asking our Lazlo to do. On second thought, maybe she did.)

"But I don't know anything about football," Lazlo demurred.

"Good," said Lance. "That's even better. You can keep everybody's mind off the game."

"Whatever you say," said Lazlo. "You've always been my idol. I sure couldn't let you down now." He couldn't let Phineas Higgins down, either. He remembered what Higgins had told him he had to do—how it would be up to him to save Tuesday Night Football from gridiron and television oblivion—and suddenly his task took on a new and scary aspect. *It's one thing to play my jingle at halftime,* he thought, *but how am I going to take over for a TV legend like Haywood Grueller?* Still, being Lazlo, he was not about to shrink from the challenge.

"Haywood," said Lance to his fallen partner, "why didn't you just say 'no'?"

Lazlo gave Haywood a sip of water from his canteen. Haywood stirred and seemed to be trying to lift himself up. It was hopeless. He was trying to say something. Lazlo leaned in closely to hear what it was. "Rosebud..." Haywood muttered in a barely audible whisper that sounded like a death rattle.

"What'd he say?" asked Yanya, who had never seen *Citizen Kane.*

"Something about a sled, I think," said Lazlo, who was also a movie buff.

But there was not time to decipher Haywood's obscure reference. They were back on the air.

"Welcome back to Soldier Field, everybody, where the score is forty-two nothing," said Lance, forgetting to say which team had the forty-two and which had nothing. "This is shaping up like a real barn-burner," he lied, "so you might as well settle back with a Lite Beer from Miller and enjoy the game." (What was there to enjoy?)

Lazlo stumbled over Haywood to get to his seat next to Lance. In his haste, he forgot to put on his headphones.

"Haywood's feeling a little under the weather tonight," Lance yawned into the microphone, "or I'm sure you'd be hearing a lot more from him right now."

"I guess it's just you and me, Lance," interjected Lazlo. "Don't worry, folks, Haywood's a little green around the gills but he's going to be fine. It was just something he ate." He turned to Lance: "Has this turned into the most boring game you've ever seen or what, Lance? Good thing we've still got all these great commercials to break up the monotony. There's absolutely nothing happening down there, folks."

Yanya doubled over in laughter and nearly choked on her

coffee, spewing a stream of the hot liquid through the broadcast booth window to the box seats below.

"I'll murder the sonofabitch!" shouted Pete, who was tearing his hair out in huge gobs. "I'll bludgeon him in his sleep! I'll torture him before I kill him!"

"Who told you to put that knucklehead on the air?!" Morton's image in the control truck monitor was apoplectic.

"He just jumped in there, Morton," explained Pete nervously. "Haywood's out of commission. You want me to cut his mike?"

"I want you to cut his *throat*, you guinea bastard!" screamed Morton so loudly that the engineer suffered permanent hearing loss.

"You're not going to cut anything," said Yanya into her microphone. She was talking to Morton Finch and she meant business.

"Who said that?" sputtered Morton. "Yanya, did you say that?"

"I said it and I meant it," she said resolutely. "You're not going to cut anything."

"Have you forgotten whom you're talking to, young lady?" Morton was not used to insubordination, especially from women. Nothing short of total amnesia could account for Yanya's sudden departure from abject subservience.

"You might be the Wizard of Oz for all I know," said Yanya, "but as of now I'm still the producer of this show and I say Lazlo stays on the air. Haywood's belly-up in the corner, Lance is dead on his feet, and Lazlo's the only thing we've got left. Not only that, he happens to be a very nice guy who had his heart set on this, and you've been treating him like shit since the minute he got here! If Lazlo goes, I go."

"That goes for me, too, Morton," said Lance. "Sorry."

(They'd both been lazloed.)

"This is the mother of all mutinies!" bellowed the most powerful man in television impotently.

"That's precisely what it is," said Yanya. "Say something,

Lazlo," she instructed, sounding very much like a producer.

"You mean you just want me to be myself?" asked Lazlo. "Say whatever pops into my head?"

"I'll pull the plug and see you *all* hanged!" vowed Morton, who tended to overestimate the social importance of television.

"You may have us hanged, Morton," said Yanya, "but you'll never pull the plug."

"Oh? And why won't I?"

"Because this is live television, and the one thing live television won't tolerate is two hours of dead air, that's why."

Morton, even for a television executive, was smart enough to realize that she had him over a barrel. The middle of the game was no time to call the bluff of his mutinous crew; he'd have to wait until after the show to fire them, or kill them, or something.

"Besides," added Yanya, "it's not Lazlo's fault that he's even here. If you want to take it out on somebody, why don't you take it out on Phineas Higgins?"

"You're absolutely right," said Morton, who seldom entertained the thought that anybody else was ever right about anything. "It's Higgins we have to thank for this, isn't it? Higgins and his little band of snot-nosed Madison Avenue jerkoffs. They all think they can fuck with Morton Finch, do they? Well, we'll see about that. I'll show *them* who runs Tuesday Night Football. We'll leave the Jingle King on. Yeah, that's it. We'll let your friend Lazlo step on his pud in front of forty million people and just see how the sponsors like *that*. By the fourth quarter Higgins'll be begging me to take him off the air."

# SEVENTEEN

**T**he game was so bad that Lazlo and Lance ran out of things to say at the same time. Lazlo decided that it might be a good idea to open up the phone lines so that the viewers could call the booth and discuss their thoughts on the game, jingles, or anything else they might want to get off their chests.

And people called. Millions of them. They called from bars and cars and airplanes. They called from home, they called from the office. All the couch potatoes in North America rose up as one, seizing the opportunity to be more than mere popcorn-munching, beer-swilling observers and become active participants in the greatest and most noble of all American pastimes, Tuesday Night Football. Wanda Pozniak called. Mirek Celinski and each of the Fabulous Polecats called. The President of the United States called from Air Force One. Lazlo's mother even called (she was in a Scottsdale jail for slugging a motorcycle policeman). Tele-

201

phone circuits were overloaded from Bangor to Honolulu, and the phone companies got richer.

"He's corny! He's crazy! He's nuts! What a fucking dildo! Jingle King my ass!" Morton was having a wonderful time wreaking revenge on the powers behind his network throne. So what if Tuesday Night Football went down like the *Titanic* with him at the helm? At least he would have the satisfaction of taking the sponsors down with him. Better to go out in a blaze of glory, he thought, than to be nibbled to death by advertising executives.

The engineer, who couldn't take it anymore, had a major nervous breakdown and was led away in restraints from the production truck by three large men in an ambulance. Pete was left to run the console by himself, and seriously contemplated suicide before realizing that no one would really care.

Meanwhile, the first half ended unnoticed while Lazlo was talking to a woman caller from Rapid City, South Dakota, about early Sioux Indian needlepoint, a subject close to Lazlo's heart.

"Well," said Lazlo as he said goodbye to the caller and looked out over the stadium, "there's nobody on the field so I guess the first half must be over. And Lance is out of it, too, ladies and gentlemen. Sound asleep up here. But I guess if you had a day like he had, you'd be dog-tired too. And ladies, let me tell you, everything they say about my old pal Lance is true. You've got Lazlo's word on that."

All of a sudden there was a great commotion outside the booth. The door burst open and Lazlo was startled to see Hoover, the FBI agent, wrestling Simon Blackthorn to the floor. Simon was carrying Lazlo's accordion and a ghetto blaster, and he didn't like being manhandled.

"Knock it off!" said Yanya. "This is no place for that. It's a network show!"

"I found this redskin lurking outside," explained agent Hoover. "He looked kinda fishy to me."

"Simon, what are *you* doing here?" asked Lazlo as he gave his friend a great bearhug.

"I told you, Lazlo, *some*body has to look after you. By the way, would you kindly tell this gentleman that there are treaties between our respective peoples now. He doesn't have to beat the shit out of me."

"It's okay, officer," Lazlo said to the G-man. "You can go now. Simon's my alter ego."

Noticing his accordion, Lazlo was nearly overcome. "Simon! Where'd you find my ax?"

"I come from a long line of trackers, Lazlo," said the Indian as Lazlo took the *Soprani* out of its case and checked for any damage. "It was lying on the side of the Dan Ryan Expressway. Looked like it had been thrown from a speeding car."

There was not a scratch on the accordion, and a great weight was lifted from Lazlo (like the time he realized that he didn't have to be cool to be happy). Having been reunited with his beloved instrument, he could not only play his jingles for everybody at halftime, but he knew he could carry the rest of the show by himself if he had to.

"Boy, this is swell," he said, and he meant it.

"What happened to *him*?" asked Agent Hoover. He was pointing to Haywood, the man he was supposed to have been guarding.

"Oh, he's just a little whacked," said Lazlo. "He'll be okay."

"Well, you can't leave him here," said the fed, who liked to assert his authority whenever possible. "He's a fire hazard."

"We'll get him out right after the game, officer," said Lazlo as he led Hoover to the door. "Right now I have to do the halftime show."

Simon, meantime, noticed that Haywood's toupee was dangling from his head by a single thread. Unable to stifle his primal Native American impulses, he leaned over and cut the thread with his buck knife and attached Haywood's rug to his scalp belt.

"That must be what the old dame was talking about..." mused Agent Hoover aloud. (He was always about three beats behind, which made him eminently qualified for government intelligence work.)

"What old dame?" asked Lazlo.

"*Ugly* old broad," said the G-man. "We picked her up trying to leave the stadium and beat a confession out of her. Said her name was Rosebud Grueller. Said she'd just 'taken care' of her ex-old man.

"Oh, well," he shrugged. "if it's only him I guess it doesn't matter. Just don't let him clutter up the place, okay?"

"I won't," said Lazlo.

Meanwhile, an interesting lineup of guests was assembled in the green room for the halftime show. Oliver North was there, dressed as Rambo. Shirley MacLaine was there, dressed as Cleopatra. So was Sylvester Stallone, dressed as Oliver North. There was also a singer named Springsteen and a career politician named Nixon. It seemed that everybody who was anybody was in Chicago for Tuesday Night Football, hoping to be seen on national television with Haywood Grueller.

But it was not to be. Lazlo was in charge now, and his moment of truth was at hand—the culmination of a lifetime of hopes and dreams for a simple Hungarian immigrant who wanted nothing more than to make people happy.

"This is it, Lazlo," said Simon. "This is what the whole country's been waiting for."

"You mean right now?" said Lazlo, who was suddenly a little nervous.

"You're the Jingle King, kimosabe," said Simon reassuringly. "Go for it."

The commercials ended and the camera was pointed

squarely at Lazlo. Yanya stood off to the side, holding her breath. She didn't know what was going to happen, or why she even cared, but at that moment she wanted Lazlo to succeed more than she'd ever wanted anything before. She'd been more than lazloed; she'd been truly enlightened, and in the process liberated from her own man-hating history. She began to have the most peculiar thoughts—fleeting visions of a future somewhere in the Arizona desert, surrounded by a brood of Lazlo babies, and it made her smile. (Why not? Stranger things have happened.)

Lazlo squeezed a few tentative notes out of the accordion and suddenly every trace of nervousness vanished.

"This is the happiest day of my life, ladies and gentlemen," he said into the unblinking eye of the camera, "and now I'd like to share with you the jingle I wrote especially for this occasion. Pete, can we pipe this out through the stadium p.a.? I'd like everybody to hear it."

"Do as he says," instructed Morton over Pete's anguished scream, which was audible all the way to Skokie. "Our ratings have tripled in the last twenty minutes." (Could it be that Morton's strategy had backfired?)

And Lazlo began to play—softly and sweetly at first, caressing the keyboard, bending the reeds—then finding a perfect rhythmic groove, his fingers flying with a virtuosity seldom seen on this or any other continent, the music swelling to crescendo with harmonic brilliance and dazzling counterpoint. He was a man totally in control of his instrument and his destiny, which were as one.

And when Lazlo began to sing his Everything, Inc., jingle he sang with such passion and conviction that everyone overlooked the fact that he wasn't exactly Pavarotti. The jingle became an anthem, plucked out of the genus of ordinary jingledom by his electrifying performance, elevated to the pantheon of the commercial pitch—a hymn of praise to the advertising deities on the order of the Song of Solomon or (at the very least) "We Are the World":

> "Everything Corporation is always on the job,
> We can help you clean your toaster,
> We can pacify a mob,
> We can do your income taxes,
> We can fell a redwood tree,
> We can even take you sailing on the bright, blue sea,
> We can even take you sailing on the bright, blue sea;
> We can put you in a pickup,
> We can help you buy a ring,
> We can book your reservations
> From Boise to Beijing,
> And our pet food division can make your birdie sing,
> Everything is Everything,
> Yes, Everything is EVERY-THING!"

In bars and taverns all across the country people began to sing along with the Jingle King, while the 64,000 fans at Soldier Field rose from their seats and joined in, clasping their neighbors' hands and letting their voices soar to the heavens as they swayed gently back and forth in the aisles. The game was delayed for forty-five minutes as the players returned to the field and, temporarily forgetting their hostilities, did the same. For the briefest of moments in the great scheme of things all of America was at peace.

They'd been lazloed.

When it was over, and play was about to resume, there was one final call. It was from Morton Finch.

"I don't know how you did it, Lazlo," he said, and this time he wasn't angry, "but you've saved Tuesday Night Football. You may be weird, but you're a genius at it. Just tell me what you want and it's yours." No one had ever heard Morton talk this way.

"I just want everybody to be happy, Mr. Finch," said Lazlo, and he meant it.

"Then you just stay with us and I'll make sure that that happens," said Morton. "I'm going to make you a star, Lazlo."

There must be a God, because that night the impossible happened: Even Morton Finch, the toughest, most ruthless man in television, actually admitted that he'd been wrong.

He, too, had been lazloed, and he has never been the same since.